It is an early morning in Texarkana. The heat index is nearly 100 degrees at 8:00 AM. The dew is so heavy on the practice fields that walking across them would soak a pair of shoes and leave footprints on the field until the sun is a little higher. Beyond the end of one of the practice fields is two old portable buildings that have been put together to form the Coaches' offices. The heat of the summer sun seems to almost cause the pores of the old buildings to open up and give of the musty sweaty kid smell that was left from the years the buildings were used as classrooms. The front of the building houses the office of the athletic department's secretary Lisa Rice. Lisa has been in that position for many years and could tell the row and seat where most people in the community sit during games. Just beyond Lisa's office is a larger room with several desks and chairs. A pair of old sneakers lay on the floor beside one of the desks. On another desk is an old wrinkled sweat shirt and an old track trophy. On the left hand wall of the coaches' office is a door with a small sign on it that reads "David Cleveland Head Football Coach and Athletic Director. The silence of the morning is broken by Lisa's voice calling out "Cleveland, remember you have a 2:00 O'clock meeting with Dr Carr." Coach Cleveland could feel his stomach going into a knot as Lisa's voice approached. Coach Cleveland responded with an indignant "Thank you". Lisa then goes on to say "Coach Cleveland, I know you look forward to these meetings about as much as you would a root canal, but Dr. Carr is a smart man. He knows that the talent level is not the same as it has been in the past and it's like you say, "it ain't the X's and the O's that win you games it is the Jimmy's and the Joe's."" She then turned and walked out of the office. Cleveland's dread is fueled by several lack luster years. Last year's football team really never lived up to the expectations of the community. Coach Cleveland had been promoted to Head Coach last year after serving several years as an assistant. He had been the Defensive Coordinator for most of those years as an assistant and his defenses were legendary. Many games in those years were won because the defense held the opposing scoreless. Cleveland has a frustrating life as a perfectionist. He is in search of the perfect defensive strategy and trying to carry that strategy out with 16 and 17 year old boys. He was also a history teacher who loved teaching in the classroom and his only regret when he moved to Head Coach was giving up his classroom duties. His passion was war and the strategies that won wars and shaped the future. His love of military strategy and discipline ran through his team. He felt that the best way to prepare kids for a football game was to prepare them as if they were preparing for battle. Often the strategies for his defense had its basis in military strategy.

Arkansas High has a rich tradition in football. The 70s saw the team win back-to-back-to-back State Championships. Several teams in the late 70's and early 80s also came close to State Championships. The community has come to expect high finishes every year from Arkansas High. During the glory years fans would fill the 7,000 seat stadium each week for home games. If there was a big game that particular week, the stadium would fill and people would line the fence surrounding the field to watch the game. Most weekends people would make plans based on where the Arkansas High game was being played. If they were in town people knew not to leave town because their plans were already made for Friday Night.

Many things have changed since those days. Dropping enrollment has decreased the pool from which the team has to draw talent. Dwindling community support and closing industries has have led to deteriorating facilities. Each year several of the best athletes will transfer to surrounding school districts that have newer facilities. In the town there are four major high schools. If an athlete doesn't want to or isn't able to play for one particular school often times they will turn in an address of another family member and attend another school in the town. Arkansas High's program once was the one where all the kids wanted to go, but over the past several years more kids have been leaving the school that coming into the program. Texarkana Texas High School has been very successful over the past few years and has been the recipient of many of the transfers from Arkansas High. The kids want to be part of a winning program, and changing schools is often the easiest way to do this. The community doesn't see the transfers they only see a program that doesn't win as much as it did in the past. The fans do not understand why the program no longer is as competitive on the state level as it once was.

The following day Coach Cleveland makes his way over to the Superintendent's office. Dr. Carr greets him at the door. Cleveland walks into the office. A beautiful oak desk sits in the middle of the room. Behind the desk are several diplomas on the wall. As always everything on the desk is in the right place even the pens are lined up. "Come in, David." They both enter the office and sit. The one good thing about being called to Dr. Carr's office was getting to sit in the nice leather chairs. The administrative building was still new and the smell of fresh paint was a far cry from the musty smell of the coaches' offices. They exchange pleasantries and discuss how each of their families is doing. Finally, after fifteen or twenty minutes of chit-chat the meat of the meeting begins to come forward. "David, do you know what makes a good school year?" inquires Dr. Carr. Cleveland fumbles around a while and then replies, "Well, good kids, good faculty, good discipline policy and facilities. Facilities are always important." Cleveland tries to figure out where Carr is going with the conversation while trying to also get in a plug for some newer athletic facilities. "Look, David. We've been friends for a long time," interjects Carr. "You know as well as I that you can take every bit of that mumbo-jumbo you get in school and still have a school year that will get me run out of town on a rail." Carr hesitated and then continued. "David, there are two intangibles that are necessary for a good school year. Number one there must be good food in the cafeteria. If the food is good the kids are happy. Secondly, there must be a good football team. If those two elements are in place my life becomes much easier. Your job David is to make my life easier. Last year my life was not easy. The cafeteria once served grilled peanut butter and jelly sandwiches. I know why they did this. The workers knew that each meal had to have a hot component and that each meal must have a meat or protein component. So what did they do? They took the easy route. They figured if they took peanut butter and jelly sandwiches, which would have peanut butter serving as the protein component and then they grilled them they would have their hot component. David, I ask you this. Have you ever been in such a bad way in your life that you resorted to eating a grilled peanut butter and jelly sandwich?" As

Cleveland began to speak, Carr continued. "I'm sure you haven't, but you have placed a team in the field that could only muster four wins. David, with the tradition at Arkansas High we've got to have more wins than four in a season." Carr hesitated again and then continued. "David, I went to all the games last year and I thought the season had ended on November the 2nd after we got pounded by Bryant High School." "Well, it was the last game of the season, and we didn't make the playoffs. So, it was the last game of the season." Cleveland replied. "David, the following Sunday morning I got up and I went to church, as I always do on Sunday morning. Most of the time church that is the one place I can go and get away from the work world. When your school has a bad football team there is no escape, not even in church. David, I sat down and the preacher began to talk about how he had attended Friday night's football game against Bryant, confidently expecting Arkansas High to win and narrowly avoid a losing season. He told how the Razorbacks stumbled out of the blocks and never really recovered. He went on to say how he was ready to leave with about five minutes left in the game when Bryant trotted that 'little midget kid' on the field. He told how Bryant's crowd stood and gave the loudest roar of the game as the kid ran onto the field. He told how he was a champion of the underdog and had to stick around just to see how it all turned out. He went to great lengths to tell how the young man first was in the huddle and then stepped up to the fullback's position. He went into a dissertation about our inability to tackle a kid who could not have been taller than a fire plug and wasn't much faster. He told how the young man brought the crowd to its feet for five minutes with a sixty yard touchdown yard that took four and a half of those five minutes. The preacher went on to say that he began to leave at that point when he passed a friend who stopped him. He told him not to leave because he had heard that Bryant was going to put in a trick dog to carry the ball the next series and see if we could tackle him. David, this was the preacher's own cute way of making a seg-way into the story about Zaccheus." Cleveland sat there not knowing how to respond then Carr broke the silence. "David, I'm counting on you to take care of one of my objectives, and if you can't take care of one objective I don't know that I can keep the school board off of you. So if you don't take care of one objective you may be taking care of the other objective, which is the cafeteria. Cleveland sat a moment and then responded, "This year is gonna be much better. We are going to put a much better product on the field." Although he had no clue of how to take a team that was 4 and 6 last year, with no influx of talent, and make them a better team.

Carr started again. "David, I know Coach Jones plans to retire in the near future and I know his plans do not include taking the teacher's exam. But David, stunts like the two that he pulled this last track season are going to force me to fire a man who is loved by the community. I understand that he is old school, but old school can go too far." Cleveland knew of at least five events last semester alone that would get an ordinary coach fired, but he also knew that further questioning into the events could bring to light three incidents that Carr apparently had missed. Cleveland just shrugged his shoulders and replied, "That's just Doc. He loves the kids as much as anyone, but he is old school." "Yeah, and if those old school shenanigans continue we will all be fired!" exclaimed Carr. David, you know I can't fire him because I would be hunted down by most of the community and I would go down in history as the man who fired a legend. Cleveland looked at Carr and said, "I can't promise anything. Doc has been around a long time and is set in his ways." "One other thing, David. Now you know I am a church-going man but we can't be playing church with your athletes." "What are you saying?" asked Cleveland. Cleveland knew what he was talking about. He had purposely brought in speakers who would say things that he couldn't as a school official and each practice and game ended with a team prayer. The coaches didn't lead the prayer but it was understood that each practice was to end by thanking the Lord for the opportunity to come out and practice or play. Carr then continued, "David, you know this is a public school and you know there are lawsuits concerning church and state throughout the country. I don't want to be involved in one of those. I want a lid put on your church playin' with the football team." The meeting broke up with Cleveland heading toward the door trying to figure out how to win the upcoming season. He wasn't worried about controlling Doc, that was really Carr's problem. "David" Carr called out. Cleveland turned around. "Tell your wife I said hello."

Cleveland returned to the coach's office to find Coach Bill Hollingshead watching game films from last season. Holly, as he was known to most was a career Army man who retired and became a coach to pass the time. He coaches the defensive backs and special teams and is a champion of the underdog. If a kid worked hard Holly would find a place for him to play. Holly spoke up in his typical gruff tone, "Well, what'd the Super have to say?" Cleveland replied, "Oh, the usual stuff. He says if we don't win he will put me in charge of the cafeteria." Without even turning around Holly responded, "Does he know we have the same weak team from last year and no returning quarterback? How do you turn dung for talent into a competitive team?" Holly asked. Dee Desrochers, or 'Coach Dee", the offensive line coach walked into the office. Coach Dee also had the responsibility of maintaining the football fields. This was the second year in a row he had over-fertilized the fields and burned the grass to bits. When mid-October rolled around, though, there would be a lush, green turf on the field, but until then the grass would not need mowing. This is why Dee is accused of purposefully doing it. Dee then said, "Hey, I heard you were meeting with Carr. Did he mention how good the fields looked last year?" Holly then replied, "He said you'd be spooning out mashed potatoes if the grass wasn't green by the first game and we didn't win at least eight games." "Did he, really?" replied Dee. "You know if the grass is green in September it will die by playoff time." "Playoff time, playoff time?" Holly and Cleveland both responded together. Then Cleveland continued, "I'd settle for a 500 season." "What, are you afraid of the Super, Dee?" asked Holly. "No," stated an indignant Coach Desrochers, "I just get tired of always being the bad boy in the group. The bad boy always takes abuse whether he did it or not." "Bad boy of the group?" screamed Cleveland. "My word, Son. Are you the one the fans are hollering to fire every time we lose? Are you the one who went 4 and 6? Are people of the community saying 'Let's fire the offensive line coach'? You don't know what bad is." The discussion continued to rage with each of the three coaches trying to top each other as to who was the baddest boy on the block until Coach Ray 'Doc" Jones walked in. Coach Ray Jones, or 'Doc' as he was known, had coached Arkansas High since integration. He was in his mid sixties and had planned to retire soon partly because he wanted to, but also because mandatory teacher testing was on the horizon and he refused to take the test. He walked slumped over, had a knot on his forehead that would actually increase in size when he had been drinking. He was an old-school coach who believed in discipline and accountability. The community left Doc alone. Most of them respected him and the rest of them definitely feared him. The nickname came about because Doc had had a secret balm that he put on injured athletes. The balm was very hot to the skin. Ben-Gay and Icy Hot could not touch Doc's balm. It was hard to tell at times if the balm really helped the players to get better quickly, or if the athletes just wanted to avoid another treatment. The office went silent when Doc entered the room and asked what he had missed. It went without saying that Doc was the baddest of the bunch. Dee then said, "Cleveland just got out a meeting with the Super." "Huh," stated Doc, "That son of a gun ain't gonna fire me because I was motivatin' my runners last year, is he?" Then Holly replied, "He ain't gonna say a word to you. He knows you plan to retire in a couple of years. He's not gonna touch you! You're Sacred! Heck, you could cut up a couple of kids, that is if you haven't already and STILL get away with it."

The previous track season had seen Doc at his finest. No one got more from their athletes than Doc. The track athletes had run poorly in the first three meets. Following the second meet Doc got on the bus with the rest of the team and shouted, "Shot putters get your shots. Discus men get your discs. Pole vaulters get your pole. Sprinters get your blocks and get off my bus!" The kids sat there stunned. He again shouted, "Get off my bus!" The kids gathered up their equipment, slowly made their way off the bus. The kids were now standing beside the bus when Doc started the engine and shouted, "Now get to running and I'll see you at the school." The meet was held at Liberty Eylau High School which was almost seven miles from Arkansas High. Doc drove the bus the entire way behind the last athlete until they all made it back to the school.

The following week saw another dismal performance from the track team. When the runners got on the bus following the meet and one of the runners had the audacity to ask "Where are we gonna eat on the way home?" Doc turned beet red and screamed "EAT, EAT?" He stood speechless at the front of the bus. He stood trying to gather himself and try to respond without going too far with his response. Coach Files was the assistant track coach and drove the bus for all out of town track meets. No one knew exactly why Doc wasn't allowed to drive, but people could offer several hundred possible reasons. Doc finally added, "Er, Files. Drive this bus over to that E-Z Mart that we passed as we were coming into town." Coach Files, not saying a word, drove the bus to the E-Z Mart, pulled up and stopped. Doc got off the bus and walked toward the front door of the E-Z Mart. His walk resembled that of the Pink Panther with a gut. He then eased his way into the E-Z Mart. Several of the kids thought he was going to get himself something to drink to forget about the meet. Coach Files would have been lying if he had said that the thought had not crossed his mind as well. Doc emerged a few minutes later with a large brown paper bag full of something. Now, Files," Doc said as he climbed back on the bus, "let's go to the Sizzilin". The bus made its way across town to the Western Sizzlin' parking lot. "Park near the window, "Doc said. The bus came to a stop. Doc stood up and opened the brown paper bag. Files thought to himself, 'He isn't gonna bring booze into the Western Sizzlin, is he?' Then Doc pulled a large slab of bologna out of the brown paper bag along with two boxes of crackers. "Landrum, Landrum! Come here." Doc called to one of his best senior runners. "Get up here!" Doc began pulling a pocket knife out of his pocket and opened up the blade. He was never without his knife. Doc often used the knife to motivate his athletes to work harder. He would never touch an athlete with the knife but he would many times show it off to get their attention. Landrum made his way tentatively to the front of the bus. Doc handed him the knife. "Now, give each one of these son of a guns four crackers and two pieces of bologna. If there is some left over after every son of a gun has eaten his meat and crackers then give the son of a gun another helping." Doc then turned to Coach Files and said, "Now Files, let's get us some real food." The coaches made their way off the bus and into the Western Sizzlin and ate while watching the kids on the bus through the window. By the end of the season Doc had taken that track team who could barely score in local meets to a third place finish in the state meet.

Doc had so many legendary stories that no coach on staff could come close to his "bad boy" image. So the coaches continued to discuss ways to improve the team instead of trying to beat a dead horse as who was the baddest. The coaches realized that part of the problem with last year's team was the fact that most starters were juniors and sophomores. The coaches hoped that all the returning players would be better because they were now a year older, a year stronger, and a year faster. The position where there was really no answer was the quarterback position. Last year's quarterback, Josh Henry, was a good quarterback but limited by the young players around him. The back-up quarterback was also a senior and had graduated. Several kids were tabbed as ones who might step up into the role, but most had never played the position, while those who had previously played quarterback just weren't very good. The first order of business when practice started was to find the kids with the most potential to play the quarterback position.

CHAPTER TWO

Dew was still on the ground at the start of the first practice. The sun was getting hotter with each passing minute. By the time the players had finished stretching the shoes and socks were soaked with the morning dew. There was a warm squishing feeling in the shoes with each step. The first day of practice always carried with it a great deal of confusion but today's level of confusion was particularly high due to the frantic search for a quarterback. A group of ten kids who had either played the position at some time in their life, or who had a burning desire to play the glory or goat position assembled to try out for quarterback. Two of the athletes were ruled out immediately because of inability to walk and chew bubblegum at the same time. Of the remaining eight players there were only three with above average talent. As the first morning practice of two-a-days ended, Cleveland, in his mind, had narrowed the quarterback position down to three athletes, but none of the three excited him. Cleveland made his way to the coach's office. The south wind seemed to blister the skin rather than cooling it. Cleveland was stopped just before he had entered the coaches' office by a man in his mid forties. The man wore jeans and a beat up tee shirt. "Coach," the man said, "I'm Jim Bridges. My two boys and I have just moved to town. My oldest one's name's Jamie and he wants to play football." Cleveland, who was still frustrated with the progress of the morning practice just barked, "Take him to Doctor Compton and get him to get a physical. Keep in mind we have a lot of good athletes here at Arkansas High who have been in the program for years, so don't expect your son to play much. He'll have to work to earn a position. Go to Lisa, my secretary. She'll give you the directions to Dr. Compton' office. Get him a physical and then we'll get him started as soon as we can." Cleveland then continued into the coaches' office. Bridges stood a moment then as Holly passed by Ed Bridges asked "Where's Lisa?" Holly then walked with Bridges and pointed the way to the office.

The first couple of weeks of practice would consist of two-a-days, a morning practice and then a second practice late in the afternoon. The second practice of the first day focused on the three primary candidates for the quarterback position. As the practice wore on

Cleveland began thinking of ways he could improve the cafeteria after the dismal season he was about to face due to lack of a skilled player playing at quarterback. He was fast realizing that none of the three would be sufficient to pull the team out of the losing rut it had so strongly established the previous year. At that moment an old beat-up truck screeched through the parking lot and right onto the grassy area next to the practice field. Jim Bridges jumped from the vehicle, and walked swiftly through the middle of practice straight up to Coach Cleveland. He jumped into Cleveland's face and began screaming, "So you think my boy is a sissy, do ya? You could've just told me that. You could've just told me you thought he was a pansy." The coaching staff and entire team stopped what they were doing to watch the fireworks. Cleveland, who for the past two weeks had been living out the worst nightmare of his life, responded, "Sir, I have never met your boy, and I have no clue as to what you are talking about." Holly began to move toward the two men while Coach Files tried to move the rest of the team to another area. Coach Files called to the players, "Men let's go through the rope run again. We gotta get use to picking up those legs." Cleveland stood staring at Bridges and quietly growled, "If you do not get off my practice field I will ensure that neither you or your boy ever set foot on this field again." Bridges was almost shaking with frustration when he retorted, "I know that you and your assistant coaches probably had a good laugh sending me to an OB/GYN clinic. I can just see you sitting in your office wondering how we would respond when the receptionist at the Dr.'s office she asked which of us needed a breast exam. So just tell me who to take the boy to see to get a physical." Cleveland stood a minute trying to keep his composure, wanting to laugh so badly that it hurt. Holly was not able to conceal his laughter as well as Cleveland. "Sir, our team physician is Dr. Compton. He is an OB/GYN. I'm sorry for not mentioning that to you, but we are very used to it. We really don't think about the fact that he is an OB/GYN. Neither do the kids. He is like family to us." Coach Hollingshead then spoke up and said, "Yeah. Just take that boy of yours over there and get him a pap smear and we'll get him started." Bridges then stood for a moment too embarrassed unable to respond. He then quickly jumped back into his truck and sped off. "I hope that kid wasn't an athlete," said Cleveland. "What makes you say that?" Holly replied. "Well, I don't expect after that episode his dad put on that the boy will show his face around here," replied Cleveland. "Oh, he'll be here, "said Holly. "His old man's a drunk. The kid needs to be on the field." "How do you know the man's a drunk?" questioned Cleveland. "I've been in the military most of my life. I know a drunk when I see one," Holly replied.

The following day arrived and the players returned with a little less enthusiasm than they did the previous day but still with a good deal of excitement. There was a new face in the crowd today. A tall, wiry kid with sandy-blonde hair named Jamie Bridges. He arrived in an old beat-up old Toyota Corona, made his way toward the locker room by following the rest of the team. The starting middle-linebacker was a young man named Keith Willis. Keith confronted every new player, "Who do you think you are?" Keith inquired. "Jamie Bridges," he retorted quickly and nervously. "What are you doing here?" "I guess I plan to play football," replied Jamie. "Well you don't look like much of a football player. If you think you're man enough you'd better see Cleveland over there." With that Keith entered the locker room. Jamie walked toward the building that Keith had pointed towards and knocked on the door. From inside the coach's office he heard several scream, "Come in!" He walked into the door of the coach's office. The wiry, blonde-headed kid introduced himself and said he wanted to play football. Cleveland responded gruffly, "You ever played before?" "A little in junior high in the town where I moved from," Jamie replied. "What grade classification are you?" Cleveland asked. "I'm a junior," replied Jamie. "What happened last year to make you not play?" Cleveland questioned. "Family stuff," Jamie quietly replied. "What position?" asked Cleveland. "Position?" inquired Jamie. "Yeah, what position on the football team do you play?" Cleveland questioned intently. "Oh, the coaches at my old school used me at safety on defense and quarterback on offense, but I'm willing to play wherever you want me to play," responded Jamie. "Well, get you some practice gear from Coach Holly and get dressed. We'll see what you've got." With that Coach Cleveland returned to working on his computer.

The locker room was wild as Jamie made his way to an area that looked like an equipment room. Loudest, he could hear Keith tell everyone that this was his year and he was going to lead them to be the best defense in the state. "Not a single touchdown. We're not givin' up a single touchdown, baby!" He could see a coach talking to one of the players in line. It was Coach Holly. The player was Jerome McAfee. Jerome was the tailback. He had started every game his junior year and was expecting to have a big season this year. Coach Holly asked, "McAfee, you know what I like about you?" McAfee was very self-confident, but in a good way not arrogant. He was obviously flattered by Holly's comments thus far and was excited to hear the good things that Holly was going to say right in front of his teammates. Several of his teammates had gathered around McAfee to hear the compliment from Coach Hollingsworth because it was very rare that Coach Holly complemented anyone. Jerome McAfee felt like this was his moment to bask in the glory while Coach Holly, of all people, talked good about him. McAfee poked out his chest, strutted and then replied, "Naw Coach. Tell me, what do you like about me?" "Not a dad gum cotton picking thing! Now get your stuff and quit walkin' around here like you're a stinkin' hostess at a cotillion!" screamed Holly. The smile that previously had adorned Jerome's face was now replaced with an embarrassed grin. "What do you want, maggot?" Holly barked at Jamie. "I need some practice equipment," Jamie replied. "Practice equipment was handed out last week and practice started yesterday," said Coach Holly. "Yes sir, I know. I just moved here last Thursday. Didn't have a physical until yesterday," Jamie replied defensively. "Was that your daddy who got all bent out of shape 'cause we sent you to an OB/GYN?" asked Holly sarcastically? "Look, he thought you were making fun of me and he didn't appreciate it. If you don't want me here just come right out and tell me. I don't have to play ball. I can find plenty of things to do to occupy my summer," Jamie responded with great emotion. "Looks like we got a live one here. I like that!" quibbed Holly. "But I'll tell you this. If you ever use that tone of voice with me again, you're mine!" Jamie stood almost embarrassed and shocked that he had responded that way to a coach, much less a coach he didn't even know. "Er, uh, Sir, I'm sorry. It won't happen again. Could I please get my equipment?" Jamie stated without looking up. "What position do you want to play?" Holly asked. "I was a safety and quarterback where I came from, but I will play whatever position you want me to." Holly grabbed the equipment then returned to the window. "Quarterback huh?" Holly grunted. "Yes sir" Jamie responded. "I hope you're a quarterback." Holly shot back.

Practice began as it usually did with the usual agility drills followed by stretching activities. They would still be in shorts, tee-shirts and a helmet for the next two days. The team was then broken into groups based on their positions. Cleveland called for Jamie, "Bridges, get over here with the quarterbacks and receivers. I wanna find out if you can play." Cleveland held up a piece of paper with a play drawn on it. "Run this play on two." Jamie stepped up to the line with only the receivers. He barked out some signals and the receivers went downfield for a pass. Jamie dropped back and threw one near-perfect pass after another. Dee walked over to Cleveland. "Hey Coach, looks like he's got an arm." Cleveland then replied quickly, "He can throw the ball when there's not eleven people breathing down my throat. Let's wait until we put on the pads to make that determination. He may be nothing more than an All-American in shorts." As practice neared its conclusion the first defense was put against the first offense to go through some schemes without contact. After several running plays Jamie dropped back to pass and hit one of the receivers over the middle. Some taunts came about the defense's inability to stop the offense. Another pass play was called and Jamie again found his receiver, and threw a strike for another big gain. Cleveland then told the defense, "We'll stop throwing when you can stop us." Three more pass plays went for big gains. The defense was totally frustrated. Indians have war cries but Keith Willis, the middle linebacker for some reason barked like a dog to show his enthusiasm. But now with the frustration his enthusiastic barking was replaced with raw anger. Keith began to push a little harder even though the team was going through non-contact drills. He began to hit a little harder and a little harder. Keith got to the point of total frustration and ripped through the line. Jamie got off another perfect strike just as Keith nailed him. The coaches screamed at Keith, "What do you trying to do, hurt the only quarterback we've got?" "Don't nobody run over my defense," Keith responded. At that point Coach Hollingshead jumped in Keith's face. "Hey, Maggot. They already ran over THE defense, and it's not your defense I'll have you know. If I knew you were a leader and thought that you could handle it, I might say it was your defense. But you know what? You're replaceable unlike the teammate you just tried to injure, you're replaceable. Now bear crawl two laps around the track. When we put on the pads you can have your opportunity to hit somebody, but not in shorts! That shows me absolutely nothing except that you're a cheap shot artist."

The first day of pads brought the first chance for the kids to scrimmage. Jamie had emerged as the obvious choice for the quarterback position and the leader of the offense. Keith Willis was going to lead the defense whether they liked it or not. Jamie and Keith led their respective units in very different ways. Jamie was not one to say more than what was totally necessary. It was unclear whether Jamie was just a silent leader or a new kid who was a little bit afraid to say too much. Cleveland tried to control his enthusiasm on the first day of pads. He knew if Jamie looked half as good in a scrimmage type situation as he did in shorts and a tee-shirt his quarterback worries were over. Cleveland called for the first offense and the first team defense. Keith was barking loudly about his first opportunity of the season to hit someone. The two teams lined up. "Bridges," Keith shouted, "you're mine, boy. It's gonna be hard to throw the ball with me on top of ya." Jamie just shook his head and called out the signals. The fist play was a running play to McAfee right up the middle. Keith immediately filled the hole and threw McAfee down for a one yard gain. "You in my house, boy! You're weak. You gotta be bad like me". The next play was a pass play. Cleveland usually would work diligently on the run offense before trying the pass but he had to see what Jamie could do under pressure. Jamie called out the signals and dropped back to pass. The offensive line gave him plenty of time and Jamie was able to find his wide receiver running an out and quickly hit him square in the hands. A sigh of relief came from Coach Cleveland. Keith hollered, "Hey Bridges, anybody can throw when there's no heat!" The next play was another pass play. Jamie again had good protection, was able to drop back and pass the ball squarely into the receiver's hands. Keith began hollering at the defensive coaches. "Call a blitz. Let me take his head off!" A blitz was called but Jamie saw it coming and changed the play to a draw instead of a pass. Jamie dropped back as if he was going to throw and just as the defense had committed to the pass he handed the ball to McAfee who popped through the line and ran to the end zone. "You wuss," cried Keith. "You're scared to throw when I'm comin' after ya!" Jamie walked to the line for the next play, looked Keith squarely in the eyes and made a throwing motion with his arm. Keith growled, infuriated about the lack of respect, but excited to know that this was his chance. Jamie called out the signals and as soon as the ball was snapped Keith tore through the offensive line and was in the backfield. Jamie was rolling right for dear life and he took a drop step and stopped. Keith went flying past grapping nothing but air. Jamie then reared back and threw a perfect spiral to a wide receiver running a post pattern. Keith got up humiliated, pointing at Bridges. "You're mine! Nobody makes me look bad!" One of the offensive players responded, "He just did, Keith!" Keith growled and walked back to the defensive huddle. "Alright, men," Cleveland called out. "This will be the last play today." Jamie took the snap and he rolled right again. Keith tore through the line and had a bead on Jamie. Jamie took the small, half-hearted drop step allowing Keith to get him by the jersey and bring him down. "Well, it's about time!" Coach Hollingshead, screamed out. Keith jumped to his feet and began barking the rest of the defense responded by barking back at Keith.

Jamie was the last player left in the showers after practice when Keith walked in and said, "Hey Bridges, you looked pretty good out there." "Thanks," Jamie replied, "you're not doing so bad yourself." Keith then looked around noticing that no one was around, "Hey, I appreciate you letting me save face out there in front of my friends." Keith whispered. "I don't know what you're talking about," Jamie responded. Keith hesitated, "You had me if you wanted me, all you had to do was move a little quicker and you were gone. Anyway, I appreciate it." Jamie responded, "Yeah, whatever."

The coaches were more upbeat with every practice. There wasn't much doubt about Jamie's ability to throw the ball and run the team. As Jamie was leaving the locker room Coach Holly asked him what he did to make him so accurate in throwing the football. Jamie replied, "I don't know, um, I guess me and my brother would play in Dad's cow pastures a lot and we would have cow patty fights."

"What are cow patty fights?" Holly asked. Cow patty fights are when you and someone else go into a cow pasture and you throw cow patties at each other. You want to get a patty that is dried on the outside but still wet in the center. Those patties will break open when it hits someone and spill its contents on them. If the patty is wet you get your hands all nasty and can't throw it. If the patty is too dry it'll only break apart when it hits 'em." Jamie then continued, "I've gotten pretty accurate throwing those things, but my brother Kevin when he's my age, he will be better than I am 'cause he's already throwing better than I did at his age." Holly thought for a moment. That's why you throw so well on the run. I guess you grew up dodging dung rather than other players." Jamie replied, "Yeah, I'd rather be hit by another player than a wet cow patty."

Coach Holly had been wondering about all the strange equipment in the back of Jamie's car. Every time Jamie drove up in his Toyota Corona he had a great deal of equipment piled in the back. The 1980 Corona's looks were definitely not its best feature. The car had a brown paint job that had faded and cracked over the years. Coach Holly moved the conversation from football to the car. "Jamie, how many miles you got on that old Corona?" Holly asked. "We don't know," Jamie responded. "I think it's 300 thousand miles, but Dad swears the odometer has rolled over four times. Well, I'd better get goin', Coach." With that, Jamie hurried over to his car and headed off. In the back of the car as he drove off Holly could see a tackle box, a bow and some arrows and an inner tube. Each day when he returned to practice the equipment seemed to be in a different place of the car, indicating that it had either been moved or used for some purpose and put back. Questions and guesses went through the coach's office each day until finally one day Doc burst into the coach's office with great excitement. "Hey, I know where Bridges' is going each day!" he exclaimed. All the coaches looked at him with enquiring looks. "After practice I headed to the spillway at Lake Wright Patman," Doc continued. "Since we had finished practice early I had a little time to kill before I got home to the wife. I was going to catch some buffalo and gar fish for the weekend. I looked around and as usual there were a bunch of people along the spillway. When I looked up I saw something strange, amongst all of us ole' folks in our lawn chairs with our cane poles was a young boy going up and down the spillway on the rocks with a bow and arrow. He would shoot and with almost every shot pull up a big gar or carp or drum. He had a reel attached to his bow and line attached to the arrow and when he would hit the fish with the arrow he would reel the arrow back in. As soon as the fish was shot the people fishing along the spillway would raise up their hand, Jamie would walk over to one of the people, there and he would give us a fish." "'Us?!'" Holly interjected, "you mean you got one?" "What are you talkin' about?" Doc retorted, then continued, "I got four or five. After he got through bow fishing he took off to check his trot line. He told me where he was headed, so I decided to follow along. I followed him down stream to see how in the world he was going to check a trot line without a boat. There was no boat or trailer attached to his car. I looked up and if you can believe this, and he was pulling the inner tube out of his car. He walked over to the water and climbed in the inner tube and then paddled himself out to the line. I never would've believed it if I hadn't seen it myself. The kid gets into his inner tube, paddles his way out in the water. He has a big, thick, orange glove that comes up to his elbow on one hand. He checks the line and there were a couple of 20 pound cats on the line." "How does he get 'em in?" Cleveland questioned with concern. "You can't get a fish to land in an inner tube," he continued. "That's the best part," replied Doc. "I'm tellin' ya if I hadn't seen it with my own eyes I wouldn't have believed it. I slipped up, and I watched as he would paddle out in the inner tube with the big orange glove on one hand. He would stop at the knot where the drop lines were and he would pull up the line. If there was a fish on it he would take the fish off the hook and he would get out of the inner tube and he would hold the fish with the hand that had the orange glove on it and hold the inner tube with the other arm. The fish would swim like crazy but eventually would wear down. Jamie, while he was holding the fish and the inner tube kicked his way back to the bank. He would leave the fish in a cooler and then go back for another one. He pulled in four fish that must have gone over 20 pounds." "What's he going to do with all of that fish?" Holly asked. "Well," replied Doc, "he gave me two, and another to a guy along the water's edge and then he took the other one home." Coach Dee perked up, "Hey, I need a big fish for our aquarium." "What? Are you saying you have a catfish aquarium at your house?" Cleveland questioned. "Not in my house" Dee shot back. "See, the Science Department has put together a small zoo for the students to see and study some of the animals that they never come across. 'Cause if it ain't got a collar on it, then they don't see it in the world they live in. I'm currently the only teacher in the department that hasn't contributed an animal to the zoo. A 30 or 40 pound catfish would make a nice addition." "Yeah, Dee. That'd be real good." Doc said. I may need the key to your room where you keep that big catfish. Ya'll ain't got snakes in there, do ya?" The conversation droned slowly back to the progress of the football team.

The coaches gathered together toward the end of two-a-days to get an assessment of the team. Now they felt they had a much clearer picture of who would start and who would play. They were also gaining confidence in this year's team. Coach Files had been at Arkansas High for the past ten years. He was past retirement age but loved coaching so much he would never consider retiring. Coach Files was one who loved the dramatics. Everything he did had to have pomp and circumstance. He stood up in the coach's office and drew three columns on the chalkboard. At the top of the first column he wrote 'catfish and hushpuppies'. Over the second column he wrote 'beans, coleslaw and tea', and at the top of the third column he wrote 'lemons'. Holly stood up and growled, "Files, what kind of dung are you coming up with now?" At that moment Coach Files had Lisa bring in a big tray full of catfish and hushpuppies. "Men," Coach Files started," the catfish and hushpuppies are for the guys who start and are going to contribute in a big way this season." Lisa then stepped out of the room and returned with Tupperware containers of beans, coleslaw and a big pitcher of tea. Files then continued, "The beans and the coleslaw and tea are the players who we gotta keep an eye on, 'cause they might be players at the end of the year. You see, the catfish and hushpuppies can stand alone, but if you got beans, coleslaw and tea, then it's really good." Lisa left the room again and she returned with a big bowl of lemons. Files, at this point, was really feeling his creative juices. He stood up and said, " And the lemons, well you really don't need the lemons for a meal, but if you've got some lemons it looks good. So, as we eat, lets fill in the columns." The coaching staff began to gather around the desk when Dee asked, "Hey, Files. Where'd you get the fish?"

"Got it from Bridges. I told him to get me some for today and he brought me in enough for all of us plus my wife and I will eat well tonight. Now, let's get down to business. Who are the catfish and the hushpuppies?"

There was a brief silence, then Cleveland said, "Well, on the offensive side of the board Jerome McAfee and Jamie Bridges are going to be able to do some damage for us at quarterback and running back." Files grabs the chalk and writes. "Bridges and McAfee. Who else will start on offense?" That crazy Knight is going to end up being our wide receiver and punter," Cleveland grumbled. Allen Knight was a very likeable kid who came from a very wealthy family. He played in the past and always seemed to get a great deal of press for anything he did. He was very fast, almost 6 feet 180 pounds. During the previous year Keith had tackled him in practice. When Knight got up he noticed that Keith had a booger on his cheek. Knight looked at Keith and said, "Hey Keith you got a giant booger on your cheek." Keith immediately replied, "That is the sign of a hard worker. You wouldn't know anything about that." Within two plays Knight had found some sour apple gum which was green and plastered it all over his face. He then after his next catch ran directly toward Keith so he would be tackled. As Keith got up after the tackle he noticed Knight's face and said "Dude what's on your face?" Knight replied, " A booger! Am I working hard enough for you now?" Cleveland spoke up again, "Farmer will be the fullback." Dee added "My offensive line will have Joey Jamison, Clay Jones, John Henry , James Jamison and Green at center." Files then said, "I like Doster and Murphy at the end. Okay, who are our beans, coleslaw and tea on the offense?" The coaches looked at several athletes that they felt might contribute as the season went on. Dee spoke up, "I think George McWilliams might help us on the offensive line." "George?" Cleveland screamed. "That tub of goo? Men, if we gotta go to war with people like George we might as well cancel the season." Dee then said, "He's a senior," to which Cleveland quickly retorted. "Yeah, Coach Files is older than the hills too. It doesn't mean I want him defending my freedom." Dee sat a moment then responded. "He can move people off the line when he wants to." "The problem is getting him to want to," Cleveland then responded. "I'll believe it when I see it." Files then moved to the offensive lemons. Several names were mentioned in this group.

Files then said, "Okay. Let's look at the defensive side. Who are the catfish, hushpuppies and tea?" "Keith Willis and Hardcastle are two of my linebackers," Cleveland spoke up and said. Cleveland, although he was on paper the offensive coordinator still had a big hand in the defense because he loved the strategy involved in defense. "What about that son of a gun, Brady? He's done as well as anyone." Doc asked. "Brady could be the third linebacker, but he's a renegade. I don't see him staying out of trouble." Cleveland replied. "He's been in trouble his whole life. We'll have to fire him before the season is over. Last year we had to fire Denton. Brady is one of his runnin' buddies." Denton was one of the most gifted athletes to come through Arkansas High but because he had so many run-ins with coaches and school officials had to finally be kicked off the team. Doc sat a moment then replied, "I think there is something more in that son of a gun. Do you remember when he came to practice wanting a box of band aids to cover the 126 stitches he had on his chest because his girlfriend took a box cutter to him. He wanted the band aids to cover the stitches so he would not miss a day of practice. Let me have him. I'll take care of him. Put him in the catfish group." The coaches continued through the afternoon until the entire list of players was listed as either catfish,/ hushpuppies, or tea/beans/coleslaw, or as lemons.

The following afternoon practice Coach Desrochers cornered Jamie. "I hear you're quite the fisherman." "It's just something I do to pass the time," replied Bridges. "If I go home Dad will put me to work. I have enough chores as it is. I don't plan to add to my workload by hanging around the house." Dee then said, "Well, as you probably know I teach biology. The teachers in the science department are trying to get together a small zoo for the school. I had the school shop class to build me an aquarium a while back but have not had any big fish to put in it. I've gotten some bass and brim, ya know the small stuff, but I want a really big, cool monster size fish. They got bored looking at the little stuff and if you'd do that for me I'd owe ya one." "Sure I will. I only catch the fish 'cause it's fun. It's cool to see people's eyes light up when you give them their supper before they leave."

The following day was another hot, tropical type morning practice. Toward the end of practice Dee approached Jamie and said, "Hey, would you be able to get me a fish or two by next practice?" "Yeah, I should. There are some clouds and the water is clear." "Okay," Dee replied. "I'll bring something to keep them in until I can get them in the aquarium. What kind of fish do you think it will be?" "What do ya want?" Jamie asked. "Oh, I don't know. I want 'em to be big and the weirder the better," Dee replied. Jamie thought a minute and said, "I think you need a big gar 'cause those things are about as ugly as they come, and maybe a big catfish. My trotline is out there and I haven't had a chance to check it today, but hopefully there'll be a pretty good cat on the line. I'll probably have to get the gar with the bow."

Jamie drove up that afternoon before practice in his beat-up old Corona. He parked in an area where the other players had parked and began walking toward the coach's office. He approached the coach's office door and knocked . Several voices called from inside for him to come in. Jamie looked in to see the coaches watching films, practice sessions so far. Coach Dee jumped to his feet when he realized it was Jamie. "Hey, how'd it go?" Dee asked quickly. "Pretty good, I think. I was able to get you a couple of pretty good fish," Dee responded. "Well where are they? Let's see 'em," Dee said excitedly. "I have them in the car in a cooler. Where do ya want 'em? Would you mind helping me carry the cooler?" Jamie asked. Dee replied quickly, "Sure, I'll help ya carry the cooler and let's take 'em to the training room and put 'em in the big ice chest we carry to the games. I can store them in there until I can get 'em into the aquarium." Both approached the car and Jamie opened the trunk. A musty, fishy smell came from the trunk as it was opened. Jamie had a large ice chest that looked as though it had been in a war. Jamie pulled the lid open and inside the cooler was filled with fish and just enough water to keep them covered. The water was blood-stained. "The cat will go about 30 pounds and the drum about 15. The drum is the one that's bleeding. I shot him in the tail with the arrow but he should be fine. I caught the cat on the trotline."

Dee stool dumbfounded at his new pets. "Man, this is great! This is so cool! Man, I owe you one!" Both took the cooler and carried it to the locker room to transfer to a larger cooler. The following day they would be in their new home in the high school science department zoo.

CHAPTER THREE

After three weeks of temperatures hovering in the mid 90's and humidity over 80% it was now time for a scrimmage game with the Hope Bobcats. Hope was a top notch 4A school while Arkansas High was 5A by classification. Even though the schools were a different classification it was usually a very competitive scrimmage between the two. The game last year was played at Arkansas High so this year's game would be held in Hope. The only hope of a reprieve from the heat this time of year is rain, but none was in the forecast. So, as always for this game it was a hot summer day. Mid-August was showing no signs of giving way to fall any time soon. The air moving from the wind was just as hot as the stagnant air. The hot air almost stung the skin. The players made their way off the bus toward the visitor's locker room. Just outside the visitor's dressing room was a well-stocked vending machine sitting up on a step. George McWilliams was a senior, an offensive lineman who had not played much his sophomore or junior year. He walked to the vending machine and stopped. George was a player Dee felt could contribute to the offensive line while none of the other coaches gave him a second look. He had not eaten since breakfast and was feeling the need for anything to eat but preferably something with high sugar content and lots of preservatives. He then asked several of the players around him for money for the machine. George's build, 5-foot-10, 270 pounds reflected his love of unhealthy food choices. George turned to the other players and said, "That is the job, right there." One of the players looked up and said, "What are you talkin' about?" "You know, "George replied, "the guy who fills the vending machines. Just think about it. Someone has to replace the candy and those snack cakes after it has either been bought or it's gone out of date. You can't tell me the dude pulls out the old Twinkies and Ho-Ho's and throws all that good food in the trash. I know the dude is probably having snacks all day long at every vending machine he changes. Man, can you imagine? Your job is to drive from one vending machine to another and eat the old food? The food's not really that old, it's just about to go out of date." George looked around at the players around him who did not seem to exactly be agreeing with his thoughts. "Don't you think that's the greatest job there is?" Keith spoke up quickly and said, "I think if you spend half the time thinking about football as you do Twinkies, you might be worth something to this team." The players filed into the locker room. Cleveland barked out pre-game instructions. George continued to dream of how good a pack of Ho Ho's would be right now. Every few minutes he'd hear chatter outside the door then he'd hear change rattling and finally hear the beeps of the vending machine buttons and people would purchase some of the contents of the vending machine. George began to almost drool like Pavlov's dogs as he heard the beeps of the buttons and the snack cakes drop into the bottom of the machine. George thought he could tell whether it was candy or snack cakes just by the sound it made when it dropped. Just as George had gone into a deep trance dreaming of the day that he was the man who would tend the machine, Cleveland hollered, "Get out there and set a tone for the rest of the season!" The entire team got up and exited. George was one of the last ones to leave and he looked at the machine as he made his way toward the field. His stomach grumbled as he moved on to the field.

Hope was the first team to go on offense. The scrimmage would have no kicking game, just offensive and defensive plays. The way the scrimmage was designed one team would get the first twenty plays on offense then the other team would go twenty plays on offense. The first play was a hand-off that went over the right side of the line for seven yards. Hope continued this much of the night. They would gain six or seven yards and then they would bog down and then only gain two or three for a while. Keith Willis, the middle linebacker showed that he would be a force all season long by being in on several of the tackles. He also had two sacks in the first twenty plays. There were many penalties as one would expect from a first scrimmage. After Hope had finished their twenty plays the Arkansas High offense had their chance. Jerome McAfee had one run that was 25 yards and another run for 15 mixed in with several runs between 5 and 15 yards. He was running and playing even better than the coaches had expected. Toward the end of the first half the second and third teamers entered the game. George entered the game with third string and was at that point not feeling well at all. It had been a long time since he had eaten and his tank needed refueling. He went out there and for the most part just kind of got in the way. The amount of time allotted for the first half ran out. Some felt the time keeper may have run the clock a little extra out of sheer boredom to try to make the first half go a little quicker. The players approached the locker room with great caution having heard legendary stories about Cleveland's half time talks. Not word was uttered in the locker room as the kids filed in quietly. As the players sat down they could hear the coaching staff getting closer and although the players could not make out the exact words the coaches were saying they could tell this was not going to be an uplifting Tony Robbins' type talk. The door burst open and the entire coaching staff entered with Cleveland entering last.

Cleveland stood in front of the room and there was a long pause. The pause was so quiet it was deafening. As Cleveland began to speak the sound of two people arguing outside the locker room became noticeable. As Cleveland continued by saying that practice time and practice intensity would increase the sound of two people arguing became louder than Cleveland's screaming. Suddenly there was a loud grunt and the sound of glass breaking. George knew the glass breaking could only be the vending machine becoming involved in some type of skirmish. Cleveland stood waiting for the skirmish to subside. Suddenly the door burst open with one of the Hope players wearing his helmet tossing what looked like his father into the room. The player followed the man and grabbed him by the shirt and tried to push him into a locker. The man suddenly got the player by the face mask, spun the kid around and wrapped the young man's hand behind his own back. The man then calmly walked out of the locker room door and as he made his way to the door coach Dee opened the door. The man turned and looked at Cleveland and calmly said "Sorry for the inconvenience. My son needs to learn some manners. All is under control now." The player's attention again returned to Cleveland. Cleveland stood in stunned silence and racked his brain for something, anything to say. He looked at the other coaches. He had, had to give many different half time talks but never one in this type of situation. After standing there for four or five minutes unable to find a complete sentence he finally said, "Let's do better this half!"

The vending machine glass was smashed and the contents lay either in the bottom of the machine or on the ground around it. As the players left the locker room and headed back on the field George lagged behind. The other players stepped around the broken glass George stooped down as if he were going to tie his shoe. He then reached into the vending machine and stuffed his shoulder pad full of Twinkies and Ho-Ho's. He was able to get about eight packages of snack cakes into his pads before trotting out onto the field. The second half was much the same as the first with a few exceptions. Jerome McAfee was running even better in the second half than he was the first and Keith Willis on defense began to really make some strides along with Brady and Hardcastle. Jamie dropped back several times in the second half and was able to complete several passes. Cleveland had purposely limited the number of pass plays not wanting to show any coaches from other schools who might be scouting the game too much of the offense. Keith was also able to get into the back field and disrupt several passing plays as well. As the end of the game neared the coaches began to clear off the benches and let all the kids play. Although George had already been in the game Coach Dee wanted to get another look at him. Dee was convinced that there was more of a lineman in George than he was seeing. Dee called out, "George, I want you in there now!" George hesitated as he was eating his third snack cake, knowing he had to hide the other five. He quickly ran over to the tape box and crammed the rest of his snack cakes into the box and ran out onto the field. As he was in the huddle he realized the best way to get back to the food was to block so well that the team scored quickly. This half was more of a game type simulation rather than each offense running twenty plays and then switching. George, realizing that the sooner they scored the sooner he got back to the sideline, became a blocking machine clearing a path you could drive a small truck through with each play. The offense quickly moved down the field and scored. George hurried off the field to check his plunder. Before George could get comfortable he heard, "Offense, get back in there!" The Hope offense had fumbled on the first play of their drive and George again quickly packed away his loot and ran onto the field determined to take care of business quickly. The coaches were stunned with his performance and began calling play after play designed to run behind him. George would open a large whole through which the back would run through and pick up 10 to 15 yards. The offense again moved quickly down the field and scored. George would then quickly run off the field to shouts of praise and slaps on the back and high-fives, but George only cared about one thing, and that was getting back to his stash of food before someone else found it. The final seconds ran off the clock. George picked up his last Twinkie package and headed for the locker room. He dressed and ate well on the ride home.

CHAPTER FOUR

The first game of the year would be against Texas High. This is as big a rivalry as there is in high school football. The hero in this game would go down in the annals of the city's history. Seniors on the winning team would get to keep their jersey. The losing team could win every other game of the season including a State Championship and still would not be able to keep their jersey because they lost to the cross-town rival. They say there are two seasons in Texarkana. The first season is the Arkansas High/Texas High game and the second season is the rest of the games. Twice in the 80s there were documentaries done on the game. WTBS Superstation in Atlanta, Georgia came and did a show focusing on how the rivalry at times splits families. The wife who had attended Texas High while her husband attended Arkansas High was featured. Another story that year was about a coach who had coached at Arkansas High and his daughter was a cheerleader at Texas High. Over the years Texas High has won about 60% of the meetings between the two teams. The game was originally played on Thanksgiving Das as the final game of the season but as the years have gone on the game has gotten shifted to earlier in the season.

The week of the "Battle of the Border" as it is called always brings in extra security from both sides of town. Throwing eggs at people, cars and houses who have an association with the opposing team is very popular during this week. Teenagers who are caught with eggs during this week in their possession will be fined $100 for every egg.

The Monday evening before the game a white paint van pulled up in front of the Texas High marquee. Two men in paint smocks got out of the van and then approached the marquee and began to climb up on the marquee with an extension ladder. The men began to take the tiger off the marquee. The marquee would post upcoming school events and on the top of the marquee has a large Bengal tiger. At the base of the marquee was a sign that read Texarkana Texas High School "Home of the Tigers". The tiger had stood on the marquee watching over the school for the past 20 years. As they began to take the tiger down one of the principals came out of the building and shouted, "Excuse me, but what are you fellas doin?" It was 6:00 P.M. and all the students were now at home. The painters replied, "We're with McAlister Paint Company. We're here to take the tiger and repaint it. The painter fumbled with some papers and pulled out a work order. "As you can see," continued the painter, "they want us to paint it this week and bring it back after the big game commotion is over." "Hmm," the principal stood a moment. The painter began again, "Can you imagine the looks on those punk's faces when they drive over here to throw eggs at the tiger and it's not here." The principal then thought a minute and kind of laughed and said, "It'd be fun to put a camera on and watch those broken hearted kids as they drive by. Well, carry on." With that the principal turned and made his way back into the school. The tiger was unloaded carefully and placed in the paint truck. Dee and Chad Fallon were students at Arkansas High and they had an uncle in Dallas with a paint truck which they borrowed. The two were cousins but might as well had been brothers. Both were in the 12th grade and had spent much of the past 2 years pulling their plan together. The tiger was taken to a local auto-body shop. Dee and Chad had originally thought about carrying the tiger to their home but with friends coming by all the time they knew someone would probably rat them out. The owner of the paint and body shop was a friend of the boys as well as an Arkansas High graduate. He was more than happy to help out by supplying some red paint, sprayers, and a location to hide the big cat. The tiger was then painted in a beautiful coat of red paint and the words 'Go Hogs' were written on the side of the tiger in white. A long discussion followed about when to return Little Red Tiger From The Hood, as she was now called. On the one hand returning the tiger Thursday night would almost ensure the tiger would be there in its red glory on Friday night. On the other hand it would only take is a couple of conversations with the right people for the principal to figure out he had been had. The final decision was made to return Little Red Tiger From The Hood late that night. After midnight under a cover of darkness the tiger was returned to its rightful place atop the marquee. Tuesday morning brought a great deal of excitement to the Texas High campus. Mr. Naples, the principal, was one of the earliest to arrive and quickly noticed a group of kids gathered around the marquee. The moment he laid eyes on the marquee he realized that he had made a mistake the previous day that could possibly haunt him the rest of his life. He could see the article in the paper, 'Principal gives tiger away to be painted' with 'Go Hogs' painted on the side. The game Texarkana Trivia, which is a game similar to Trivial Pursuit, would probably add a question card asking 'Who was the principal that allowed the tiger to be painted red?' Within twenty minutes the police had arrived and descriptions were taken of the painters, but Dee and Chad were a step ahead. One of the boys' mother was a beautician. The boys had borrowed two good toupees. Dee had also ordered a beard from one of her magazines while Chad had ordered a very real looking moustache. The wigs were both brown while the boys both had blond hair. Both also wore sunglasses. The descriptions given to the police matched a couple of Arkansas High students but not Dee and Chad. The newspaper and three local TV stations arrived at the school at 9:30 a.m. and the whole situation was made worse by a slow news week. The red cat made the front page of the paper and was the lead story on two of the three news stations. The CBS affiliate ran it as the second story. To save embarrassment the administration of Texas High quickly tried to secure a painter to restore the tiger to its old glory. Being unable to obtain a marquee painter on such short notice the tiger was taken down and taken to the art class. The battle cry for the art students was 'Restore the Glory' and by Thursday the cat was restored to her previous splendor and returned to the marquee with a layer of visqueen wrapped around it.

The rest of the week was filled with a great deal of hype surrounding the game. Cars would cruise town adorned with, shoe polish. Many cars had slogans such as 'Eat more pork' or 'I'd rather die than go to T-High'. State flags would fly out of the backs of trucks tailgates. Both coaches would make the civic club circuit and tell local businessmen what they could expect to see not only this Friday night but the entire season. Coach Shifty James, the head coach at Texas High was a fiery coach with an old-school mentality. Several years ago after a loss to Arkansas High his team began practice at 8:00 a.m. the following morning and most of practice was spent with players running bleachers until Coach James got tired of watching them. Coach James stood before the members of the rotary club and explained what everyone already knew. He told those in attendance how this season he had the most talented group of athletes to come through Texas High in a long time. The senior and juniors of the Texas High team had been prepped for the last three years as being the group of athletes who could win Texas High's first State Championship. Coach Cleveland then got up and began to talk by saying, "This is a good group of men who will work for you day in and day out." He continued by saying, "This is a group I could go to war with. This group of young men may take their lumps but they'll not run into fox holes and hide. The younger businessmen really did not respond to his metaphor but the older men in attendance were riveted to their seats by the talk of battle and fox holes.

It was always a relief when the game day finally arrived. Each school has the largest pep rally of the season. Coach Doc Jones will be brought in at the end of Arkansas High's pep rally and sing 'That Old Razorback Spirit'. It is a song sung to the tune of 'Give Me That Old Time Religion'. Coach Cleveland then made his way to the microphone. This is the only time during the pep rally that the gym will be quiet. Cleveland pulls out the local paper and he turns to the second page. This is the page where they have the Pig Skin Picks. The Pig Skin Picks is the section of the paper where the sports writers put their picks on who they think will win the area high school, college and pro games that week. He reads, "Pig Skin

Picks game one Arkansas High at Texas High." The students cheer loudly. He continues, "Ed Scott picks Texas High." This statement is met with boos. "Larry Moser picks Texas High." More boos. "James Williams picks Arkansas High." The students then cheer loudly. James is the sports writer who covers Arkansas High. Cleveland continues, "Tim Noel picks Texas High, and Rick Simmons picks Texas High." The kids continue to boo. Cleveland continues, "These men may be right." There is a gasp and a silence from the crowd of students in the gym. He restarts by saying, "Texas High has as much talent as any team around. They have two Division-I prospects in the offensive line and a Division-I kicker. But the writers didn't take one thing into account. They didn't take heart into account. Why did this country defeat the British in the Revolutionary War? Did they have better weaponry? There was silence. Did they have better training? More silence. Did they have more talent? The answer to all of the above questions is 'no'. The reason," he continued, "is that the early American settlers had more heart. Heart won then and heart will win tonight." A resounding cheer went up, the band began to play, and the kids stormed onto the gym floor and danced as the band continued. After things calmed down the two captains came forward. Keith Willis made his way to the mike and paused a moment and then began barking like a dog. The crowd barked back at him. He stood there nervously and said, "We're gonna whoop the snot out of them." The crowd then went wild as he made his way back to his seat. Jamie Bridges then walked to the mike. The crowd cheered again. Jamie did not like having to get up and speak before a crowd. He fumbled with the mike a couple of seconds and then said," This is gonna be as tough a test as we're gonna have all season, but we're gonna beat 'em." The crown cheered loudly and the band began to play and the student body rushed down to the gym floor and began to sing the alma mater.

That afternoon the players got dressed and loaded onto the nearest two school buses on campus. The police escort preceded the bus over to the Texas side of town. As the busses approached Texas High's stadium came into focus. The stands were made of concrete and the stadium was built for football only. There was and had never been a track around the field at Tiger Stadium. The stadium was abuzz with local news media setting up for the game. The turf at Texas High Stadium was always immaculate. The grass looked like a fairway of a golf course. No track around the field meant the bleachers of the old concrete stadium come within ten yards of the field. When the crowd is into the game it feels like the crowd is right on top of you. Both teams completed their pregame activities as the sun slowly sets over the home team's bleachers. The crowd gets to their feet for the National Anthem, school alma maters and the pre-game moment of silence. They remain on their feet cheering as the teams enter the field. Every male in the stands who played in the Arkansas High/Texas High game relives the day that they ran onto the field for the game. Men who did not play in this game dreamed of what it would feel like to run onto that field. Keith barked like crazy as Arkansas High ran on the field. He would bark three times solo then the team in unison would bark back.

Arkansas High won the coin toss and was on defense first. Texas High tried a long pass play on the first play of the game and the ball fell incomplete. On the second play they handed off to their big tailback who met Keith at the line of scrimmage and was crushed to the ground. Keith began barking like a dog. Texas High tried to throw again and it was incomplete, so Texas High had to punt to Arkansas High. The ball was punted and Allan Knight received the punt and was immediately tackled. Jamie and Jerome led the offense to the field. Jamie nervously looked around and then called the play in the huddle. He called out signals, took the snap and handed off to Jerome who tore through the line for a 4 yard gain. Jerome walked back to the huddle saying, "They can't hold me tonight, Baby!" Jamie got a laugh and the nervousness left him. The following play Jamie rolled out, looked up field and threw the ball for another 12 yard gain. The crowd came to their feet. Jamie & Company continued to grind the ball toward the end zone but as they reached the Texas High 30 yard line penalties and a few busted plays caused the drive to bog down. Jamie came off the field as the punt team went on. Leaning over the rail as Jamie went to the bench was his dad who had obviously been drinking. He was hollering that if the rest of the team wasn't going to help him that Jamie just needed to throw it or run every play. Jamie looked at him feeling the eyes of the entire stadium watching him and his dad rather than the game.

Jamie quietly said, "Yes Sir," and put his index finger to his lips as if to shush his dad. His dad then spouted back, "Don't you shush me, Boy! I have every right to say what I want. Do you hear me?" "Yes Sir." Jamie quietly responded as he sat down next to Jerome McAfee on the bench. "Is that your old man?" Jerome asked. "Yeah," replied Jamie. "Do you ever just wanna tell him that if he is so bad to bring himself down on the field?" "Yeah," Jamie replied. "I'd like to tell him a lot of things." The conversation was suddenly interrupted by Cleveland with a marker board drawing out plays. Jamie and crew went back out on the field. A couple of pass plays moved them to the Texas High end of the field, but as before the closer they got to the end zone their drive would stall. First down run for 2 yards had started the series then the offense jumped off sides leaving second and 13. Jamie threw a little out route for 10 yards leaving a third and 3. A Counter play to Jerome netted 2 ½ yards leaving fourth down and a foot. The following play called was a blast to Jerome. Both teams crowded the line. The crowd came to its feet knowing this was the first big play of the game. Jerome took the hand-off and ripped into a hole. He was hit by a linebacker and spun hoping to fall forward for the first down. Jerome suddenly looked up and there was nothing but green grass between him and the end zone. Texas High had crowded the line and once Jerome ripped past the first wave of defenders he was alone. He burst past the line of scrimmage and down the fields. No thoughts, just instinct. Just get to the goal line. He ran feeling and hearing nothing. As he crossed into the end zone the mute button was suddenly turned off and the noise was deafening. Jerome jogged to side line trying to be calm and act like it was no big deal. As he approached the side line Keith was barking and said, "Jerome, I know you're about to bust, just let it out!" Jerome screamed and jumped up and down in one place. The extra point team ran onto the field and kicked the ball through the uprights. So the first quarter ended. Arkansas High leading 7 to 0. Arkansas High for the start of the second quarter kicked off to Texas High who moved steadily down the field and drove the ball all the way down to the 6 yard line of Arkansas High. They handed off to one of their big backs who spun off of a tackle and into the end zone making the score 7 to 7.

Texas High kicked off following this touchdown and Arkansas High fumbled the ball on their own ten yard line. Texas High quickly recovered and scored making the score 7 to 14 in favor of Texas High at half-time. The players made their way behind the stadium. The visitor's dressing areas are as bad as the field is good at Texas High. The dressing rooms are made of cinderblocks. There are very small windows at the top of the walls. Looking out a window will allow you to see the tops of trees and the sky but not much else. The building was long and narrow like a wide hallway with no other rooms. Since this was the first game of the season it was a pretty good bet that no one had been in the building since last fall. As the players entered the dressing area the heat and humidity became almost suffocating. When Cleveland entered the building he shouted let's get out of here and marched the players to a grassy area just beyond the end zone that was being used as a parking area. The second half began with Arkansas High receiving the kick. They moved from their own 20 to their own 40. The drive then stalled and they had to punt the ball away. The two teams battled up and down the field throughout the third quarter but neither team was able to net any points. By the start of the fourth quarter many of the players were feeling the effects of the near 90 degree temperature and high humidity. Texas High began the fourth quarter with a strong drive down to the Arkansas High 30. Texas High then threw an incomplete pass and then on second down picked up 4 yards. On third and six they attempted a draw play that was stopped for a 3 yard gain. It was now fourth down and two on the Arkansas 23 yard line. Rather than attempt a long field goal the Texas High coaches decided to go for it. The quarterback took the snap, turned and handed off to the tailback who saw a giant hole in the middle of the line. As he reached the line of scrimmage he was met by what he felt like was a wall. The play was stopped for a 1 yard gain and the ball turned over to Arkansas High. Following the play all the players got off and ran off the field except for Keith. Coach Dee ran out on the field to check on Keith. As he got to Keith he asked, "Hey Keith, are you alright?" "I'm straight," replied Keith. "Well, what's hurt?" Dee asked. "Nothing," Keith replied. Dee began thinking that maybe Keith had a concussion or something along these lines and asked Keith, "Were you hit in the head?" "No," replied Keith. Then Dee asked, "Okay, what day is it, Keith?" The crowd was sitting quietly and impatiently. "Friday. Why do you ask?" Keith replied. The official was standing near the two and began to giggle. Dee's frustration began to show as he screamed, "Keith, why am I out here?" "I don't know, Coach." Keith replied. "Look, you little punk. Why are you still sitting on the field?" Dee screamed. "Oh, that. Well, I figure after a hit like that you need to sit down a minute," Keith replied. Dee then turned and walked off the field as the referee laughed so hard he began to shake. Keith got up and followed Dee and as they approached the side line Cleveland asked, "Hey Dee, what's wrong with Keith?" Dee paused a second and then said, "I don't know, you ask him." Cleveland then turned to Keith, "Say Willis, you okay?" "Tough fellow like myself? Yeah, I'm straight," and Keith walked over to the bench. Arkansas took over the ball on downs with seven minutes left to play in the game down by seven points. On the second play from scrimmage the right guard from Arkansas High went down with cramping in both hamstrings, a by-product of the heat and humidity. Dee called for George, "What do you mean putting in George?" Cleveland questioned. "Coach, nobody on the offensive line performed better than George in the Hope scrimmage," Dee replied. "There's a big difference between Hope and Texas High," growled Cleveland. By this time George had made it to the huddle. Arkansas slowly moved the ball down the field mainly from the legs of Jerome picking up three and four yards each carry. The drive began to bog down at about the 27 yard line of Texas High with three minutes left. On fourth and seven Arkansas High called a time-out. Jamie and the offense came to the side line. Dee reached and grabbed George as he stood near the sideline. "George, you're holding your own out there, but you're not blowing anybody off the line like I saw you do at Hope. What's the deal?" "I need something to motivate me," George replied. Holly pops over about that time. "See this foot, boy? This should be motivation enough!" Cleveland quieted everything down and says, "Look. A field goal does us no good. We need a touchdown." He looked at Jamie and called a play, "Roll out with one receiver running the flag and another receiver running an out ten yards down the field. "All we need is the out. We'll take the deeper pass if it's there but don't force it. This is do or die men. If we give them the ball back they'll run out the clock." The crowd came to their feet as the teams re-entered the field of play. Jamie barked out the signals and took the snap and rolled to his right. Big George stumbled forward knocking down two of the Texas High linemen in his wake. Jamie felt the rush coming from the back side but had enough time to spot a receiver down the field running an out. He laid out the pass and was dragged to the ground just after he released the ball. Knight then caught the pass and was pushed out of bounds. A cheer went up from the Arkansas side of the stadium. The referee signaled first down and the chains were moved. The first down play was a pitch to McAfee around the right end that picked up two yards. Second down and 8 on the fifteen yard line with two minutes and forty seconds left, Jamie handed the ball off up the middle to McAfee for another two yards. A time out was called and the offense gathered around Cleveland who said, "Okay men. We've got two plays to get six yards with two minutes and some change to get into the end zone." The coaches were arguing over what to run. Much of the coaching staff wanted a pass play while Cleveland seemed to want to keep it on the ground with McAfee carrying the ball and Kyle Farmer the fullback on offense and outside linebacker on defense blocking for him. Farmer was not very fast and for the position of linebacker and was much too small at 5' 10" and 190 pounds, but Kyle had two loves in his life. One was hunting and the other was football. He pursued each of these passions with every ounce of energy in his being. Coach Holly walked over to the huddle at that time and said, "Just run the ball down their throat!" Then Cleveland said, "Men, we have one time-out left. If we don't make the first down on this play immediately call a time-out." The teams lined up and the referee blew the whistle to start the clock. Jamie took the snap. Farmer hit into the line with McAfee right behind him but both were stopped as if they had hit a wall for only a three yard gain. Arkansas High immediately called a time-out. The players again gathered around the coaches. The assistant coaches brought water over to the players. The coaches decided to run it on fourth and three. Farmer looked at the coaches and said, "I'm sorry that I didn't clear McAfee much of a path. It was my fault and it won't happen again." Cleveland looked at the players. "Either three yards or it's over men." The players re-entered the field of play. Jamie took the snap and handed the ball to McAfee. Farmer cleared a huge path as McAfee moved into the hole but then slipped and stumbled and fell to the ground on the 8 yard line, 1 yard short. The Texas crowd went crazy while silence fell on the Arkansas side of the stadium. McAfee just laid there. Jamie walked over and grabbed him. "Come on, let's go. It isn't your fault. A couple of decent plays on my part and this game is never this close." Texas High took the ball and knelt down twice and the remaining amount of time ran off the clock. The Arkansas High team sat in complete silence for the remainder of the game. The team went to mid-field to shake hands with the opposing players as the time ran out and watched Texas High as they celebrated. Some of the Arkansas High players just sat in silence while others walked silently to the bus. All of the players realized, although deep down they had thought they had no chance to win, tonight they had let a game that they could've and should've won slip through their hands.

CHAPTER FIVE

The week after the Texas High game is always hard whether you win or lose. After the Texas High/Arkansas High game there is often a let down by both teams from the players. The game this week for Arkansas High will be against the Liberty Eylau Leopards. Liberty Eylau is another high school located in Texarkana. The Leopards won a State Championship two years ago but have only had moderate success since that time. Although Liberty Eylau is a local team the rivalry is nowhere near as intense as the Texas High/Arkansas High rivalry. The week of practice begins and Coach Dee approaches George and asked, "You know what I saw in the Texas High game film?" George didn't answer. "I saw the old George," Dee continued. "I pulled the game film from the Hope game back out thinking maybe in that scrimmage I just thought I saw you crushing them when really I didn't. But in that Hope scrimmage you were a different man than you were in the Texas High game. In the Hope game you were tearing holes in the defensive line. In both games it was you, George. But I don't understand how you turn it on and turn it off. You turned it on for Hope and turned if off for Texas High. What's the deal?" "Coach," George replied. "It's all about motivation for me." "You said that in the game," Dee replied. "What in the world are you talking about?" "Well, it's like this Coach. You may not have noticed but when that vending machine was broken at Hope I took all the contents I could stuff under my uniform and hid it on the side line. I hid the stuff while the game was going on, and well, I don't know, I guess it kind of motivated me to play to harder knowing that between series I could get over there and be able to eat something." Dee stood in disbelief. "Now I can die," he said, "'cause I've heard it all. You're saying that if someone supplies you with Hostess snack cakes you will play better? Right?" "Yeah, Coach. I just need a little motivation," George replied. "Okay, George. I'm gonna call your bluff on this one. I'm going to go into the head coach's office and I'm gonna call my wife right now, and I can guarantee you she will have a box of snack cakes in the stands ready to give to you if and only if you blow Liberty Eylau off the line this week." "Consider it done." Geoge replied.

The Liberty Eylau game began with each team going three plays and punting the ball away. Liberty Eylau got the ball the second time began one running play after another right up the middle, each play netting four to five yards the through the Arkansas High defense. The coaches were screaming for Keith and the rest of the defense to tighten up. The barking that was so persistent from Keith during the pre-game was no longer heard. LE had moved deep into the Arkansas High territory and finally scored. The Arkansas High offense came right back. Jamie hit two passes that went 15 and 20 yards. McAfee followed Farmer through the line and got the ball down to the Liberty Eylau 20 yard line. The play stopped with an injury time-out. Clay Jones, the Arkansas High guard on the offensive line went down with a broken right ankle. "George," Dee called out. George bounced up beside Dee. "George, it looks like you have your chance to see if motivation works. My wife has the goods in the stands." Both Dee and George look up to the stands. Dee's wife looks back at them and jumps as if suddenly remembering something. She bends forward and brings up a box which she holds over her head. "You won't be disappointed Coach," George said and then trotted onto the field and assumed his spot in the offensive huddle. The play was called, Jamie took the snap and they ran a fullback counter to Farmer right behind George. Farmer hit the line and ran for 15 yards before being dragged down by the free safety of Liberty Eylau. First down and ten from the Liberty Eylau 15 and they again ran behind George. McAfee hit the hole hard and crossed through the line for 8 yards down to the 7 yard line. They continued to pound the ball on the ground and finally scored. The score was 7 to 7.

The next offensive possession saw Liberty Eylau take the ball and drive 30 yards to the 50 yard line and then had to punt. After receiving the punt Arkansas High went to passing. Jamie rolled right and found Allen Knight, the punter and receiver for a 20 yard gain. A couple of more pass plays and they moved in to the LE side of the field. McAfee was then given the ball behind Farmer and ran into a hole George had cleared then McAfee broke to the side line and scored. Liberty Eylau re-gained possession and again moved the ball steadily down the field through the middle of Arkansas High Defense. Coaches were screaming at Keith to get up in the hole and make some tackles. Liberty Eylau moved to the Arkansas High 15 and Keith went down holding his knee. He began screaming, "My knee is dislocated!" Coaches ran out and after visiting with Keith the coaches realized Keith had no intention of putting weight on the leg. "Carry my off! My knee is dislocated!" Keith continued to scream. Keith was helped to the sideline and Dr. Compton began to examine his knee. "Keith, there is no swelling and the knee is not dislocated. Where does it hurt?" Dr. Compton pushed and prodded all over the knee. Keith was distracted watching the play on the field. "Keith, where does it hurt?" Dr. Compton said loudly. Keith jumped to attention and replied, "Oh, all over the knee, Doc." His focus again returned to the field. Dr. Compton began poking and prodding harder on the knee. Keith doesn't notice as he is caught up in the game. Suddenly LE scores and Keith's focus returns to his knee. "Oh, Doc, it's killin' me!" Keith stated. Dr. Compton touches his knee as he gets up from checking it and Keith winces and screams, "Oh, it hurts right there!" Dr. Compton leans back over and begins touching the same spots he did earlier. Keith now winces and moans with every touch. Dr. Compton gets up and walks away. Holly asks, "Doc, is he gonna be okay? Do we need a pad for it?" Dr. Compton paused a minute and said, "If you're going to give him a pad put it on his head, that's where the problem is."

As Keith continued to sit on the sideline Arkansas High continued to play as they had practiced all week. They were the same team that had played Texas High but just more lethargic. The scoreboard showed a game that was very close but the frustration was that Arkansas High could blow the game wide open if they could only wake up and now the chief motivator on the team was on the bench with an injury. It was still early September and the night again was very hot and humid. The athletes had been instructed to drink plenty of Gatorade to help keep them from cramping in the second half. Managers also were sent to the concession stand to get pickle juice from the jars that that had held the large dill pickles. Cleveland had seen articles on how pickle juice might help with cramps. The second half began like the first half with both teams running three plays and then punting. Jamie's dad had just arrived at the game and stumbled to the rail. He began hollering Jamie's name. Jamie had seen his dad walking up and tried to ignore him hoping his voice would just drown into the crowd. It seemed as if the crowd got quieter as his dad got louder. Finally Jamie turned and looked back thinking this was the only way to get him quiet. A scene had already been made but hopefully he could keep it from getting worse. Lynn hollered, "What in the world are you doing on a team that can't even beat Liberty Eylau? Those guys can't beat 2A teams." Jamie then motioned for him to be quiet. "Don't you tell me what to do, Boy! What, are you ashamed of your old man now that you play with this team that can't even beat the 'high and mighty Leopards'?" Two security guards had made their way close to his dad and looked down at some of the coaches as if asking what to do. McAfee was sitting next to Jamie. Coach Holly walked up to McAfee and pretended to be talking to Jerome. He looked at Jerome and said, "Bridges, I am not going to do it without your permission, but I can have security officers take you dad and let's say get him a cup of coffee and help him sober up." Jamie then replied, "Coach, I don't want him to go jail. He doesn't mean anything by it. He just for some reason has to get drunk," Jamie replied. His dad continued to rant and rave over the rail. "He won't go to jail, son," Holly replied still pretending to talk to McAfee. I'll have them take him to the old coach's office behind the dressing rooms. They have a coffee pot in there. Security officers can take him there and sit with him until he calms down." His dad began to curse and Jamie looked as his dad and said, "Okay Coach, whatever needs to be done." Holly then motioned for security to take him around to calm down. The game continued into the 4th quarter. The Arkansas High offense went back on the field. A reverse to Greg Moore was called. Greg was back-up wide receiver and was the fastest player on the team. Jamie turned after taking the snap as if he was taking the ball around the left end and then slipped the ball to Greg. Greg took the ball and sprinted across the field and turned a corner and sprinted down the field. Once Greg had a step on the Liberty Eylau defense no one was going to catch him. He sprinted to the end zone, dropped the football and continued to run all the way into the locker room grabbing his left hamstring. Arkansas High then added the extra point making the score 21 to 14, Arkansas High. Cleveland turned to Dee and asked, "Where's he going?" "I don't know," replied Dee, "but I think he tore a hamstring." "Sprinters and pole vaulters,"

Cleveland added, "you can never depend on sprinters and pole vaulters. They are always hurt. Go check on him. I don't want someone else to find him rolling around in the locker room suffering while we're watching the game." Dee jogged down to the locker room and looked around. "Greg!" he called out. "I'm in here." Dee heard from the bathroom area. "Are you okay? I mean, did you tear your hamstring?" asked Dee. There was a bit of a pause. "Not exactly," responded Greg. "Well, what's the deal? What's wrong with you?" Dee asked.

"Well Coach, you see, it's like this. During half time I drank a bunch of Gatorade and it kind of messed up my stomach. I took that handoff and turned the corner and once I started up field suddenly I knew I had to go to the bathroom something fierce! I couldn't decide whether to fall down and pretend to be hurt before I lost it or if I should just lose it and score the touchdown. I knew we needed the points so I just went with it. I'm cleaning up now." Dee had been giggling through the whole story and said, "Son, I'm proud of you. You went and took one for the team. I mean you literally took one for the team. Do you get it? Do you get it, Greg? Do you get it?" Greg just kind of grinned back at Coach and said, "I get it. I'll be out there in a minute. Let's keep this between us, okay?" Neck went back to the sideline. Cleveland asked, "Is Moore okay?" "Yeah, Coach. He's fine. He had to go to the bathroom really bad. He'll be right out."

Having seen the touchdown, Keith jumped to his feet and began barking. He immediately grabbed his helmet and ran to Coach Holly. "Coach, I can go! Let me go!" Keith returned to the game. The game was now well into the 4th quarter and Arkansas High was still clinging to a 21 to 14 lead. Liberty Eylau had the ball and was steadily moving down the field at 3 to 5 yards a play. Nothing fancy, just smash-mouth football. Again, after one of the plays Keith remained on the field, screaming. As coaches ran out on the field to check on him Doc asked, "What's wrong boy?" "My shoulder's broken!" Keith screamed back. The coaches worked with Keith a few minutes. They eased him off the field. Dr. Compton pulled his pads off on the sideline. "It doesn't look like you've got anything wrong with you." "Oh, it's bad Dr. Compton!" Keith replied. "I think it's broken or dislocated or something." Dr.

Compton went through a complete assessment. Every touch as well as every movement of the shoulder caused Keith great pain. With only two minutes left Liberty Eylau had moved the ball to the 10 yard line. They continued to batter the middle of Arkansas High Defensive line. With a minute and twenty seconds left in the game the Leopards punched it into the end zone. They lined up for a 2 point conversion. Keith gets up, runs past Dr. Compton and runs through the coaches. "Let me go in, okay," he screams. "I'm okay! I'm okay!" He begins moving his shoulder violently in all directions. "I'm fine! I'm fine!" Dr. Compton gives the okay for him to go back in the game. "Well get in there, 'cause they're coming right at you! Get in there and plug the hole!" Liberty Eylau called a time out to discuss exactly what to run. Arkansas High was up 21 to 20. Both teams then came back onto the field and lined up. Liberty Eylau ran the ball right up the middle of the defensive line as it had all night. Keith stepped into the hole and was run over at the 1 and the Liberty Eylau tailback fell over him into the end zone making the score 22 to 21 Liberty Eylau. The Liberty Eylau players broke into celebration and ran off the field as the Arkansas High players slowly walked off.

Arkansas High would have one last chance. After the kick the offense took the field with a little over a minute left in the game. Jamie dropped back to pass and threw the ball to Allan Knight who moved the ball to the 35 yard line. They line up again and Jamie throws a pass to tight end Ryan Doster. The pass bounces off his hands incomplete. 44 seconds left in the game and the ball on their own 35. Jamie takes the snap and hands it to Jerome. Jerome breaks through the line and picks up 4 yards up to the 39 yard line. The clock clicks down to 33 seconds left before Arkansas High calls a time out. The Razorbacks are faced with a 3rd and 6. Jamie drops back to pass and finds Ryan Doster across the middle. He is grabbed and wrestled down a yard short of a first down. Another time out is called with 19 seconds on the clock. There are now no time outs remaining for Arkansas High. On 4th and 1 Jamie sprints to the right and plans to either throw a short dump pass into the flats or run it around the end and out of bounds for a 1st down. He runs around the end and sees Ryan Doster with a step on his man down field. He throws a strike and Ryan catches the ball on the 15 but as soon as he reels in the pass the defender from Liberty Eylau grabs him and strips the ball away. There was a mad scramble for the ball and Liberty Eylau recovered. At that point all Liberty Eylau had to do was kneel down and allow the remaining time to run off the clock. The players moved off the field into the locker room. Coach Dee's wife moved down to the rail and called for George. George walked over and she handed him a box of Twinkies. "George," she said, "you played a great game even if we did lose. "Thanks," George quietly responded trying to hold back a grin of pride. Several other players, especially those who had not played noticed the special treatment. A few of the parents and fans also were wondering why the snack cakes were handed out.

After taking a shower and dressing Jamie moved to his car. The players had all parked their cars on the practice field to keep them safe during the game and as Jamie walked to his car he noticed a solitary figure. He realized it was Coach Cleveland and he walked over and asked, "What are you doing Coach?" "What does it look like I'm doing? I'm enjoying the night air and the good life," he responded sarcastically. "It's gonna get better, Coach," Jamie said with confidence. "Hold it. Hold on one minute. Just how in the world is it going to get better? We're 0-2. We're one game from starting conference and the only thing we seem to be able to do is find a way to lose. Where do you get off telling me 'it's gonna to get better'? And by the way, it doesn't look like your life is exactly a dream world either. I mean I haven't seen your dad sober yet, and your mom, at least as I know, hasn't been at a game or practice." Cleveland realized after blurting this out that he had gone too far. Jamie stood in silence. "Mom died of cancer three years ago. Up until that time Dad was pretty cool. He didn't drink and he was almost always a great guy to be around. After she died he began to drink and then we moved here to get away from the memories." Cleveland stood shaking his head, "I'm sorry. Deep down I know there's more to life than football but after nights like tonight I lose touch with reality. I'm sorry about your mom." "I know it's gonna be okay, Coach. Because the Bible tells me if I do things the way God wants me to do them he'll take care of me. Coach, you do things right with this team. We pray and there is no cussing by you, the players or the coaches and you spend a lot of time talking to us about how to be good people and not just good ball players. If you continue to do things right everything will eventually work out." The conversation was broken by the sound of Jamie's dad's voice. "Jamie, get over here!" he called. Jamie looked and saw his dad with two security officers and Coach Holly. "They say you gotta take me home, Son." Jamie began to walk toward his dad but stopped and suddenly looked back at Cleveland and said, "Things may not get better tonight but I think they will eventually." Then he and his dad climbed into the old beat up Corona.

CHAPTER 6

The following Monday Cleveland spent much of the practice emphasizing that Arkansas High was a much better team than Liberty Eylau. The players moved into the film room and began reviewing the film of the game against Liberty Eylau. Play after play Cleveland would tell players, "See, no intensity." At one point he stopped the film and said, " And you, Keith, usually you are all over the place. I am usually trying to figure out how to keep you calm. Heck, I can remember games where you were like a blind dog in a meat house, but you are non-existent on this tape." "What do you mean, Coach? Listen to that! Do you hear that?" Keith asked. "What?" replied Cleveland. "That barking! Can't you hear the barking? That's me barking. I'm the one gettin the team going Coach!" Cleveland looked at him squarely. "Oh, so what you are saying is that instead of playing with a great deal of intensity, you're barking to motivate your teammates?" Cleveland asked. "Well yeah, Coach. I don't do it for my health," Keith replied. Cleveland sat a minute in dumbfounded silence, then said, "Men, we've just gotta have more intensity. Our next opponent is Fort Smith Southside. Traditionally Southside is a team that is very sound fundamentally. They have a good passing attack. Southside, as has been the case over the last five years is again ranked in the Top Ten in the State." Trying to improve the offense's play Jamie would get Farmer, McAfee and several other receivers after practice and continue to work on plays and passes on their own. Sometimes it was pass routes and on other days they focused on running plays. The players would always spend time after practice on one particular play that Jamie referred to as 'the game breaker' or quarterback special'. He told the others that when in a bind it is a play that will go for 6 points.

The Southside game began as a battle of the defenses on the first few series. Finally Arkansas High mounted a good drive from the Southside 30 yard line. McAfee followed Farmer through a hole and scampered into the end zone, the first score of the game. Just after half-time the score had changed to 14 to 7 in favor of Arkansas High. Southside, although they had only scored once, was beginning to gain some momentum. None of the Arkansas High players would say it but they were thinking about the past games when the momentum began to shift and the games seemed to just slip through their hands. The offense for Fort Smith was beginning to roll. After a draw play Keith laid motionless on the ground. Coach Dee eased out to check on him. "Keith, what's wrong?" "Coach, I'm blind!" he replied. "Blind? What do ya mean, Keith?" "You know, Coach. I can't see! I'm blind!" he spouted back. "Did you get some sweat in your eyes and make your vision blurry?" Dee asked. "No Coach, I'm blind!" Keith insisted. Keith began to sit up and look around. "Keith, did you get mud in your eyes?" Dee continued. "No Coach. I got knocked blind!" Keith said looking around. "'Knocked'?" Dee asked, "What do you mean 'knocked'? Were you hit in the head, Keith?" Keith paused a moment then said, "Yeah, yeah, yeah. I was knocked in the head! I was knocked in the head! Yeah, Coach. That's right!" Keith said. Then Dee said, "Well, okay Keith. We need to get you to the sideline." He helped Keith to his feet and began to move toward the sideline. Dee reaches out his arm as if to guide him since he was blind, but Keith just walked on. He got to the sideline and several players were in his way and he stopped to wait for them to move and then walked on. Then he sat at an empty space at the end of the bench. As Dee followed, Cleveland asked, "What's wrong now?" "He's knocked blind," Dee replied. Dr. Compton then walked over to Dee and asked, "What's wrong with Keith?" "Uh, Doc, um, he says he's blind." Dr. Compton hesitated a minute and then asked, "So how did he get to the bench?" "Well, Doc. I don't really know." As play resumed Dr. Compton began to check on Keith. Southside moved the ball into Arkansas High territory and just as the offense seemed to be about to score they fumbled the ball away. Arkansas High quickly recovered and began another drive. After struggling for a few yards on the first three plays they again were faced with a punt situation where they had to punt the ball away to Fort Smith. Allan Knight stepped back and lined up as the punter. The snap from the center was a poor snap, but Knight was able to field the snap but he was not going to be able to get the punt away before having it blocked. He quickly evaded the defender and took off with the ball. He quickly moved down the field for a 20 yard gain and a 1st down. This was the break Arkansas High needed. The fans were on their feet. Jamie and the rest of the offense trotted back on the field. Jamie took the snap and found Knight on a deep post pattern. Knight caught the ball as one of Fort Smith's defenders grabbed him by the jersey and was about to bring him down. He turned and made a quick pitch to Ryan Doster who was down field trying to help block. Ryan then took the ball further down the field and was finally tackled on the 6 yard line. Two plays later Arkansas High powered into the end zone and went up 21 to 7. Keith ran over to the coaches and said, "I can go! I can go!" Dee looked at Keith and then looked at Dr. Compton. "I thought you were 'knocked blind'." "I'm better," Keith replied. "I can go, Coach! Let me go!" Keith was hollering. Holly walked over. "You get out there and hit somebody and if you stay on that field, you better be dead." Keith then re-entered the game barking like a dog. The defense took the momentum that the offense had started with and ran with it. They proceeded to shut down Fort Smith and the offense then added another touchdown. Before the game was over the score ended at 28 to 7. Following the game, Dee's wife again called to George. As he made his way toward the rail she tossed him a box of Twinkies. Several of the other parents had noticed Dee's wife doing this at the LE game had brought their own box of Twinkies and were throwing them to some of the other players. The other players, mainly the ones who had not played much of the game, scuffled over the boxes of snack cakes. Once all the boxes were divvied out, the players then headed for the locker room to celebrate their first win of the season.

Chapter 7

The following Monday, just as practice was beginning Cleveland called Keith into his office. "Keith, come in and sit down." "But Coach, practice is about to start," Keith replied. "I know that, Keith, but I just want to visit with you for a little while." Keith sits down nervously, afraid of what is coming next. "Keith," Cleveland starts, "I want to tell you a story." "Okay Coach, I like stories," replied Keith. "Keith, there was this young man. This young man was a shepherd. His job was to make sure the sheep were fed and taken care of and no harm came to them. This particular shepherd was a good one. He would take his sheep up on a hill near the town where they lived and he would graze the sheep up on that hill on a grassy area. Each day the boy would look down on the sleepy town and began to wonder what it would be like to shake up the town. He began to think how funny it would be just to stir up the town folk just a little bit and get 'em all riled up. One day, the curiosity got the best of them and he decided he would scream that there was a wolf coming. So he stood up, looked down over the town and screamed, 'There's a wolf coming to get the sheep!" The town folk all turned. They saw him screaming and they grabbed their pitchforks. The shepherd watched the whole incident, just laughing as hard as he could. He sat on his rock falling back and forth. When the town people finally reached him they saw there was no wolf, just the sheep and a shepherd boy laughing." Cleveland continued with the story, noticing that Keith was wide-eyed and hanging on every word. Keith's face would react with every turn of the story's plot. Cleveland noticed the story had gone on far longer than he had wanted, and knew they both were missing practice, but he felt like it was worth it if he could get his point across to Keith, so he continued with the story. He continued to tell the story finding himself almost feeding off of Keith's excitement. He began to really play the story up. He got to the end of the story and told how the wolf actually did come, but the fourth time when the shepherd boy cried wolf and there really was a wolf, no one came. Then Cleveland paused, gave a long, dramatic pause, then looked at Keith and said, "And do you know what happened next, Keith?" "No, Coach," he replied with his eyes wide open. "Well, Keith. The sheep and the shepherd boy were ravaged by the wolf. The town folk found them dead on the hill the next day when they didn't return home." Keith sighed heavily. Cleveland paused a moment and said, "Now, Keith., do you know why I told you this story? Do you get what the moral of the story is? You know, Keith. What does the story mean? Can you tell me that?" Keith thought a moment, almost as if trying to calm down after being on such a high from the story. "Yeah, Coach. I know what you're tellin me. Yeah, Coach. You're tellin me that if you're the wolf you gotta be bad, and you know how I bark, so I gotta be a wolf. Coach, I ain't gonna be a dog no more! I'm changin. I'm gonna be a wolf, and I'm gonna be bad!" Cleveland sat in stunned silence. He had just spent a portion of his practice time telling this story and was faced with either wasting more time trying to re-tell the story, or he could cut his losses and move on. So he grabbed Keith, swatted him on the back and said, "That's exactly right, Keith. Be the wolf!" Keith then ran out on the field howling and screaming "I am the wolf" to begin practice with the rest of the team.

This week's game would be against the Benton Panthers. It would be the first conference game for Arkansas High. At the end of each practice Jamie, Jerome and the receivers again would gather around talking, working on trick plays. One day after practice Holly walked in and asked Cleveland, "Do they need to be staying out there after practice like that?" Cleveland thought a minute, then responded, "Well, if they leave then they might go get in trouble, so as long as they are not burning down the facilities I can't see it being a bad thing. If they want to practice a little extra, that's fine." Cleveland paused, "By the way, just what are they working on?" Cleveland asked. "Aw, some trick play they call 'the game breaker'," Holly replied. "What does it look like?" Cleveland asked. "I don't know," Holly said, "haven't really seen it." Cleveland sat a minute playing with some game films and said, "I'll make sure to slip out there some time and get a glimpse. I'm interested to see how crazy it is. Probably some kind of flea-flicker with multiple pitches and things that are too dangerous to be run." As the players were finishing up their extra practice drill, Dee walked up to grab Jamie and said, "Hey, that fish looks great in the aquarium but I have another favor to ask of you. Do you hunt too?" "Yeah, sure." Jamie replied. "I haven't really been hunting anything here lately but every once in a while I'll go out on what I call a 'critter kill' to keep my skills sharp." Dee asked, "What in the world is a 'critter kill'?" Jamie then replied, "A 'critter kill' is when you go out in the woods at night and you kill anything that moves, as long as it's legal." Dee then said, "Man, I'd love to have some animals to go along with the fish you gave me." "What kind of animals?" Jamie asked. Dee thought a minute and then replied, "Well, nothing big like a deer or anything like that, but something you typically don't see close up." "I'll do what I can." With that Jamie headed out to his old beat up Corona and headed home.

That night the moon was bright and Jamie and his brother decided to go out for a critter kill after they had finished their homework. They killed several small animals such as nutria, skink and a mole. As they were headed home an armadillo came walking across the road. The armadillo stopped and stared right in the headlights of the car. Jamie handed the wheel to his brother and got out of the car and ran out behind the armadillo. The armadillo was still fixated on the white beams of light and didn't move. Jamie crept up on the armadillo and grabbed it by its tail and began running back to the car with the armadillo frantically moving its four legs. Kevin screamed, "You're not getting that rodent in the car with me!" "Shut up and drive!" Jamie screamed. "He won't be in the car." So Jamie climbed in the car while holding an armadillo by the tail out the window. The rodent's legs were going a mile a minute. Kevin said, "What in the world are you going to do with that?" Jamie sat quietly a while, then replied, "I really don't know." They got back to the house and Jamie was still unsure what to do about the critter. He looked around and carried the armadillo all over the place trying to figure out a place to put it. He finally came to an old out-building that was on the property and tossed the armadillo into the out-building. He went and got a bowl of water and a couple of hot dog wieners to leave for his new-found friend to eat. The following morning Jamie got up and went to get the armadillo. The out-building began to shake and a horrific sound came from the building. The racket continued for almost twenty minutes when Jamie finally emerged with the armadillo in one hand looking as though he had been in a fight. He then climbed into the Corona hanging the armadillo out the window and drove to school. He arrived at school with only enough time to get dressed out and onto the practice field. Arkansas High held their football class during the first period of school so the players would get there at 8:00 and until 9:00 they would either watch films, go over some strategy for the game, or go out and do a few basic plays. Then they would come back at 3:30 after school for their full-blown practice.

When Jamie arrived several players had already made it out onto the field and Jamie quickly ran into the dressing room and because he could find no other place to put the armadillo he shut the armadillo in the dressing room's bathroom. Both doors were heavy and opened to the inside so they wouldn't accidentally come open. The restroom was big enough for the armadillo to roam, and since practice was going on no one should be going in and out of the restroom for the next hour or so. Jamie quickly dressed and went out to the practice field just in time to begin practice. That morning the defense spent a little time walking through some of their defensive schemes to ensure they understood them. The defense finished their part of practice, and the defensive coaching staff went into the coaches' office to view some practice films. As they walked, Doc turned to the others and told them he would be stepping into the bathroom in the locker room and then would come and watch the films with them after he had taken care of business. Doc eased into the locker room then opened the door to the bathroom, pulled out a newspaper from his back pocket, lit up a cigarette. Since smoking on campus was prohibited he wanted to make sure that none of the smoke remained in the bathroom afterwards so he turned on the ceiling fan, sat down and got comfortable. The pungent smell of the locker room combined with the smell of a bathroom used by 100 teenage boys and rarely cleaned would keep any administrative personnel from coming to that part of campus anyway. As he sat he could hear a scratching sound in the room with him. He thought it was just the large box fan that was blowing the smoke out of the room. The scratching noise continued. He finally looked under the wall of the next stall and saw what he thought was the largest rat that he'd ever seen. He suddenly jumped to his feet with his trousers still around his ankles and tried to run out of the stall. He quickly swung the stall door open which hit him and knocked him backward into the porcelain toilet, where he struck his head and was knocked unconscious. Practice continued to wrap up out on the field and the coaches didn't miss Doc thinking he was spending extra time in the restroom. As the players walked into the locker room, Jamie quickly went into the bathroom to get the armadillo. As he looked down he found a groggy Doc slowly coming around and the armadillo walking around on the other side of the room. As Jamie shook Doc, Doc began scrambling and screaming, "Kill the possum! Kill the possum!" Jamie quickly left Doc and grabbed the armadillo by the tail. As the entire team began to gather around, Jamie held up the animal and said, "This isn't a possum. This is a 'possum on the half-shell' otherwise known as an armadillo." When Doc saw this he said, "Son of a gun. You brought that critter in here?" Jamie replied, "Yes Sir. It's for Coach Dee's biology zoo." Doc began to pull a knife out of his pocket and move toward Jamie. "Son of a gun, I will teach you to bring an animal in here!" The other coaches began to pile into the bathroom and pulled Doc away from Jamie. As Doc was being dragged off to the coaches' office, he said "Boy, you're mine! You're mine, boy! And you owe me a big mess of catfish!" Dee walked up about that time, "Hey, is this for the zoo?" "Yeah, replied Jamie. He got hung in my headlights last night while I was on a critter kill." "Aw, man! This is so great!" Dee replied. Bring it to my truck. I borrowed a cage a friend of mine uses for his hunting dogs. It's in the back of my truck. We'll load it in there." They loaded the armadillo in the back of the truck and Jamie asked, "Um, what about Doc?" Dee laughed and said, "I'll get you off the hook. You took care of me and I'll take care of you." As Jamie went into the locker room to get changed Dee called out, "I think I can get you out of everything except the catfish," said Dee. Jamie smiled and said, "The catfish will be no problem."

The afternoon practice ended and Doc called Jamie over. "You'll be staying with me after practice today." The other coaches and players made their way back into the locker room. Doc stood with a stop watch, turned to Jamie and said, "Alright. Get off your shoulder pads and your helmet. You're going to run quarters until I get tired." So Jamie lined upon the track and ran his first quarter and Doc held the stop watch. As Jamie came across, Doc screamed, "That's not fast enough!" Jamie ran three more quarters and at that point Jamie doubled over breathing as hard as he could breathe, looked up at Doc and said, "Coach, I don't have another quarter in me. I'm worn out." Doc then began to reach down into his pocket and he pulled out a pocket knife. Doc's hand shook. Although he had not been diagnosed with Parkinsons , everyone felt that he had some of the early symptoms of it. He shook as he reached into his pocket and began to open a knife and pull it out. Doc then looked at Jamie and held the knife up to his chin and said, "Son of a gun, you know them son of a gun's that are fighting wars over in the Middle East. They be fightin them wars, they be shootin and runnin and suddenly they get tired. They think, 'I can't run another step' and they sit down on a rock and set that gun down beside them. Then suddenly the enemy comes runnin over a hill and they all have guns and suddenly that son of a gun can run like a deer! Ya see, the human body can do many things when subjected to pressure." During the time it took to tell Jamie this story he had re-gained enough energy to run a couple of more quarters. He ran two more quarters and then again doubled over and said, "Doc, I can't do any more." Doc looked at him and said, "Alright, I'll let you go but you still owe me a mess of catfish." Jamie turned back and said, "Done. No problem!"

Benton came into the game undefeated. The teams Benton had played thus far were not known for being powerhouses. The first half was a nip-and-tuck game which left Arkansas High leading just before half time with a score of 14 to 7. The second half began with a long march down the field by Arkansas High. The bulk of the yardage was covered by running plays to Jerome McAfee. To keep Benton off-balance there was an occasional pass thrown. By the end of the third quarter the score was 21 to 7 Arkansas High leading. Arkansas High kicked to Benton. The second play after the kick-off Benton fumbled the ball away and Arkansas High recovered. As Jamie ran onto the field Cleveland called out a running play for him to run. Jamie called the play in the huddle and as he got to the line decided to go for the kill. He called what is known as a 'hot color' which was green and changed the play at the line of scrimmage to a pass play. The pass was to be thrown to Knight who was running a post pattern. Jamie took the snap and faked the hand-off to McAfee. Benton was expecting the run oriented team to keep running McAfee right at them. By the time Benton realized it was a fake hand-off

Knight had run ten yards down the field and was headed toward the goal post. Jamie found him, threw a strike and another touchdown. The Benton team, although they were still on the field, mentally had gone to the dressing room. Jamie made his way to the sideline and the first one waiting for him was Cleveland. "What was that?" Cleveland asked. "Well Coach, I got to the line and I knew they were expecting a run. If we could get another touchdown very quickly the game would be over." "Who told you you were supposed to think out there?" Jamie walked back to the bench dejected. Coach Holly walked over, "Bridges!" Jamie braced for another tongue lashing, "Yes Sir," he said in a shy tone. "I don't believe I've ever seen a high school player who knows the game like you do. That was one of the best calls I've ever seen. That call changed the game from a struggle to a blow-out." "Wish Cleveland felt that way," Jamie replied. Holly leaned over and said, "You tell anyone I said this and I'll deny it and then come after you, but Cleveland is just mad cause he wasn't the one who made the call." Then Hollinshead walked off.

After a few minutes the offense was summoned back onto the field. Benton had driven a few yards and then punted. As Jamie ran onto the field Cleveland grabbed him and called the play and said, "No changes. I'm the coach." Jamie replied, "Yes Sir," then ran on the field. Coach Holly walked over to Cleveland, "Give the kid a break, David. If he's not out there you're thinking about cafeteria work and the rest of us coaches are trying to figure out where we're going to work next year." Cleveland stood a minute in silence then grunted and then walked off. The game played out to a 35 to 14 win for Arkansas High. There was a big celebration in the locker room as Cleveland walked in. He looked over the players and said, "Men, this is a big first step toward a conference championship. You're really coming together, although you still have a long way to being a good football team, you're making good strides. But men, this is only the first step. Enjoy the win this weekend, but Monday starts a new week and a new team we'll face, so be ready." Cleveland looked around looking for someone then his eyes caught Bridges. "Bridges, I want you sitting next to me on the equipment bus on the ride home." Sheer pain and dread came over Jamie as he showered and changed preparing for the bus ride home.

The buses were loaded and began to roll out of the parking lot. Cleveland looked over at Jamie and said, "Bridges, that was a great call out there tonight. Let's do this. Unless I say regardless you can change the play. I'll tell the ones bringing the play into you regardless if it's a play I don't want changed on those plays you'll have to face me if you change them. On the others I'll have enough confidence in you that if you see something you can change the play. Jamie grinned from ear to ear and said, "Okay Coach." At that moment, Coach Hollinshead, who was sitting directly behind Jamie and Coach Cleveland on the bus leaned forward and said, "Alright men are you through with your make-up kiss and hug and love fest?" Neither one of them replied. Then Holly continued, "Bridges, I hear you like to do a little huntin and fishin." "Yes Sir," replied Jamie. Holly then said, "I want to see what kind of hunter you are. You wanna go squirrel hunting with me tomorrow?" Jamie said, "Yes Sir, I'd love to." "Well be at my house at 6:00 sharp tomorrow morning." He then went on to describe the location where he lived and how to find the house.

The following morning arrived and it was 5:50. It was a crisp, cool autumn morning. Jamie drove up to Holly's house and found it just as he had described it the night before. He walked up the sidewalk to the door even in the darkness he could tell that the yard was well kept and the house was immaculate. He could see some lights were on but was afraid to wake someone up so he lightly tapped on the door. Holly arrived at the door, "Come in," he said gruffly. I've got to get a few more things and then we'll be ready to go. Come in, here, have a seat," Coach Hollinshead said. Jamie came into the den and sat down on the couch. Hollinshead, as he walked back to the bedroom called to his wife asking for a particular jacket. At that point Coach Holly's wife, Judy, walked out from the back room calling back to him saying, "It's in your closet." She walked over to Jamie and said, "I'm Coach Holly's wife, Judy. It's very nice to meet you." Jamie stood up and shook her hand and replied, "I'm Jamie," he hesitated then said, "Nice to meet you as well." Judy then continued, "I feel like I almost know you. Holly has told me a lot about you and I see you every Friday night at the games. You are quite a good football player." Jamie replied,

"Thank you." At that point they both heard from the bedroom, "I found it." Then Judy turned to Jamie and said, "Have you eaten breakfast?" Jamie replied, "I had a pop tart on the way out of the house." Then Judy went on, "Where are all your supplies?" Jamie looked puzzled at her and said, "Well, this is my gun and these are my shells," Judy then replied, "No, no, no. Where is your snack, your breakfast and your coffee or hot chocolate for out in the woods?" Holly walked through about that time, "Oh, Judy," he said, "just let us go hunting." "Now, Holly, you just wait one minute," she replied. It won't take me but a minute to whip up some sausage and biscuits and some hot chocolate for him to take out there with him." She then looked at Jamie and asked, "You do like sausage and biscuits, and you do like hot chocolate, don't you?" "Well, yes Ma'am," Jamie replied, "but I really don't want to be a bother." "It's no bother," replied Judy as Coach Holly growled. "Now you boys just sit tight a minute and I'll get it for ya." Judy went off into the kitchen and began cooking. As she began cooking, she hollered back, "Now Holly, you don't like being hungry while you're out hunting and his mother probably wasn't able to get him a snack this morning. You just let me do this." Coach Holly then replied, "Judy, his" then Jamie suddenly interrupted and said, "No Ma'am, she wasn't. I rushed out of the house too quickly this morning." "See Holly," she replied, "us ladies have to stick together or you boys would starve." A couple of minutes later she emerged from the kitchen with several sausage and biscuits wrapped up in aluminum foil all in a brown paper bag. She also had a thermos full of hot chocolate. She then looked at Jamie's clothing and said, "Oh, my. Are you going to be warm enough in just those clothes?" At that point Holly grabbed Jamie and said, "Let's go or we'll be here all day!" and they walked out the door.

As Jamie and Holly drove, Holly broke the silence. "We're going to some of my family's old land today. They've got a nice set-up up here. You'll see several deer stands. They keep the trails pretty beat down. We hunt a little bit of everything down here – deer, squirrel, turkey, even hogs from time to time, if you like to hunt hogs. We just try to kill the hogs we come across. We don't hunt 'em or anything. If we come across them we go ahead and kill 'em because they'll tear up everything you own." They arrived at an old cabin that was well preserved. Holly and Jamie climbed out of the car and walked to the area they were planning to hunt. The sun was just coming up over the horizon. Holly said, "We'll work our way to my favorite area. I never come out of here empty handed when I hunt in this area." After about an hour of walking, Holly had killed two squirrel and Jamie had killed one. As they made their way through the woods Holly saw two trees whose canopy had grown together. Right where the limbs of the two trees intersected there was a nest. Holly held up his arm and motioned for Jamie to stop and he pointed up to the nest and whispered, "I'd bet my best huntin' dog that nest has a squirrel sittin on it. I'm gonna push this tree to try to get the limbs to try to spread apart. As the nest begins to break apart the squirrel is gonna run either down that limb or down that limb," pointing up to the limbs in the tree. "Be ready with your gun 'cause a squirrel's gonna come runnin' out." Jamie aimed his gun toward the nest. Holly began to push the two trees apart. The nest began to move but no squirrel. Holly then pushed harder and still no squirrel. Then he gave a big shove and the two limbs came apart breaking the nest in half. Falling out of the nest toward Holly's head was the biggest squirrel they had seen all day. Holly was looking up frozen in fear knowing that the squirrel was about to hit him in the face. With the best case scenario the squirrel would land on his head and only scratch him up as it tried to get away. The worst case scenario the squirrel would attack and maul his face before running off. As the squirrel seemed to descend in slow motion Holly closed his eyes. There was a loud bang and the squirrel was sent flying in another direction. Holly opened his eyes and realized the squirrel had not landed on him. As he looked he saw the dead squirrel lying on the ground. Holly then looked and saw Jamie smiling with his gun at his side. Holly looked at Jamie and said in shock, "Did you shoot that squirrel off my head?" "Oh, yeah," said Jamie, "Don't give me that much credit. "He was still way up there when I got him." Holly stood in stunned silence. After a few minutes Holly looked at Jamie and said, "You shot a squirrel that was falling toward my head, Son. You could have shot me!" Jamie looked at him and said, "Naw, Coach. That squirrel was still way up there. Coach, I'm not about to let a squirrel come after my coach. No Sir! Not if I can do somethin' about it." Holly then replied, "Bridges, how do I know you weren't trying to shoot me?"

Jamie then looked at him and said, "Coach, I can't believe you said that! You're gonna make me feel bad. Coach, you saw what I did to that squirrel that was falling through the air. If I had wanted to shoot you it wouldn't have been nearly as tough as shootin' that squirrel." The ride back was quiet. Both were tired from the game the night before and hunting that morning. They spent much of the time snacking on the food Coach Holly's wife had sent. When they arrived at Holly's house the two began to unload the truck. Holly's wife, Judy, came out to help and asked about the hunt. Holly reached into the back of the pickup and pulled about five squirrels. "Two of these are the ones I killed and two of them are ones Jamie killed, and this is one that almost cost me my life!" "Aw, Coach," Jamie replied, "You're closer to death driving in your truck down the road than with a squirrel coming after you, that is if I'm there to protect you." "Protect me?" Holly screamed. He hollered in a joking manner, "What I want to know is who is going to protect me from ole' trick shot Billy here?" he said pointed at Jamie. As they went into the house Holly began to recount the story exaggerating greatly how his life was in great danger and how he could feel the bullet race by his head. Each time he exaggerated his wife shook her head and said, "Oh, Holly. Leave the boy alone." Judy Hollinshead then turned to Jamie and said, "You have to have lunch before you leave." Jamie replied, "No Ma'am, I couldn't impose." She replied, "I insist. My feelings will be hurt if you don't stay." So Jamie stayed. Judy fixed lunch. Jamie just ate quietly during the lunch not talking a whole lot but responding whenever questioned. After lunch he got up and Coach Hollinshead walked with him to the door. Jamie turned to him and said, "I really appreciate being able to spend time with you and your wife. It's been a long time since I felt part of a family." Holly then replied, "You often shoot at your family members, do ya?" Jamie laughed and walked out to his car. As Jamie walked out and climbed into his car, Judy walked up behind Holly and said, "Awfully proud of your new quarterback, aren't you?" Holly paused a minute and said, "If we had a boy I would've hoped he'd be just like that kid.

The following week would be a game played against Lake Hamilton High School. Lake Hamilton was a high school built on the outskirts of the town of Hot Springs. The students at Lake

Hamilton are usually more of the financially more affluent group. Lake Hamilton's football team is typically a very fundamentally sound football team with above-average talent. A typical year will see them finishing third or fourth in conference. Their team has never been a powerhouse in the conference, but on any given night they could upset most any team in the conference and win. When a team plays Lake Hamilton they have to prepare for everything. They can run the ball as well as throw the ball.

Just before the game the Lake Hamilton spirit groups including the band and drill team put on quite a show. Most schools you attend will put on a nice half-time show but Lake Hamilton typically will put on a pre-game and half-time show. Families will often have small tail-gate parties outside the stadium before the game. As the game kicked off the first quarter of the game against Lake Hamilton was pretty much uneventful with each team battling back and forth, but neither one scoring. During the opening drive of the second quarter Arkansas High drove the ball down the field mainly behind runs made by Farmer and McAfee. Arkansas High would be a much stronger team than Lake Hamilton and therefore would probably run the ball more and try to power it down their throat during this game. The drive in the second quarter finally culminated with a touchdown run from McAfee. Lake Hamilton received the following kick-off, ran three plays then had to punt. Arkansas High took the ball again and again punched it into the end zone for a 14 to 0 lead in the second quarter. Lake Hamilton received the following kick-off and the first two plays from scrimmage netted a single yard. Lake Hamilton faced a 3rd down and nine. There were still four minutes left before half-time. Coach Holly walked over to Cleveland and said, "We hold 'em here and punch in another one these guys will quit and the game will be over." Cleveland just grinned knowing Coach Holly was right. The Lake Hamilton quarterback took the snap, rolled out under the pressure and finally ran out of bounds for a two yard loss. After clearly stepping out of bounds Blake Brady lowered his head and hit the quarterback. A flag was thrown for unnecessary roughness and Lake Hamilton was moved 15 yards up the field giving them a 1st down. Cleveland began to scream at Blake Brady and pulled him off the field. As he got him to the sideline he continued to chew him up one side and down the other. Brady replied, "I was only trying to make the play, Coach," to which Cleveland screamed, "You make the plays on the field. Anything off the field may cost us the game." Cleveland then continued, "You've done this at least once every other game. You were flagged for it two weeks ago and you should have been flagged for it last week!" "I'm just aggressive, Coach," Brady replied. "If you can't control it I don't want you on the team!" Lake Hamilton with the help of the penalty were able to put together a drive just before half time and punched the ball just across the goal line making the score 14 to 7. At half time Cleveland was livid. He knew that if had we held Lake Hamilton on that penalty play we would have received the punt and probably scored again making the score 21 to 0 at half time, but instead he was locked in a battle at 14 to 7 with a team that could very easily sneak up on them and beat them in the second half.

The half time talk centered on not being able to put teams away. Cleveland hollered, "You had the team on the ropes and our linebacker, who decides to hit a quarterback when he is at the bench," then Cleveland paused, looked at Brady and screamed, "I just wish for once, Brady, you'd hit somebody in the field of play like that!" Brady suddenly interrupted, "Get off me, Coach!" Cleveland paused and then thought a minute and said, "Look, Brady, why don't you just gather your stuff and get out of here?" Brady suddenly jumped up and ran toward Cleveland, "No, Coach, no! You can't do that to me. No, don't kick me off. I've got nothin' else, Coach. Don't take me off the team. This is the only thing I've got. I'm sorry, I'm sorry! Let me stay, Coach. You gotta let me stay!" Tears began to well up in his eyes. "Please, Coach, I don't know what I'll do. I've got nothin' else!" Cleveland leaned over and began to whisper in Brady's ear. "Look, Son. If you want to stay on the team you need to be an asset to us. Lately you've done nothing but hurt the team more than you've helped us. I can't allow you to ruin a good season for the rest of the team. That's my job." Brady pulled back and looked at Cleveland and said, "Give me a chance. I promise, I won't hurt the team, but you can't kick me off. I won't mess up again." Cleveland stared at Brady for what seemed an eternity and then said, "One chance. Don't blow it." The second half saw the defense completely shut down Lake Hamilton. Brady played the second half like a man possessed. It seemed as if he were in on every play and was a part of every tackle made. Arkansas High's offense got a couple of quick scores in the second half and by the end of the third quarter the game was put away.

Following the game several of the coaches, including Cleveland, were going to ride back in the equipment bus. The equipment bus was much smaller than the bus that carried the team. Usually one of the coaches drove it and a few coaches would ride on it as well as a few managers and a few football players. The rest of the bus was earmarked for all the helmets, shoulder pads, jerseys and equipment needed for the game. Cleveland and several other coaches would ride the equipment bus because it would leave while the players finished eating the post-game meal. The kids would change into their street clothes following the game and load their pads on the equipment bus. As the players loaded the equipment on the bus they would grab a sack of food. Cleveland would usually pick out four or five players to ride on the equipment bus. He had two reasons for having players ride with him on the equipment bus. The first reason was to get to know the kids on the team a little better. They had more time to talk and it being a small bus they could all talk together without interruption. The second reason was that someone had to unload all the equipment. Cleveland, this week, as he handed out the sacks of food asked Jamie, Jerome McAfee, Keith Willis and Blake Brady to ride on the equipment bus home with him. During the early part of the trip home Cleveland talked about the game. He talked with each player about what he liked and did not like about the game and each individuals' performance. The last name he called out to discuss the game with was Blake Brady. "Brady," Cleveland stated, "I'll be honest with you and I want you to be honest with me." The other players pretended not to be listening but they were hanging on every word. Cleveland continued, "I did not expect you to stay on the team this year. I expected you to be gone by this point in the season. I knew you could be a good linebacker, but I also know that you can't seem to stay out of trouble. But you surprised me tonight. I fully expected you to quit me at half time and go home. You typically aren't one to hang in there. If someone makes you mad you either quit or you fight. That's what I expected you to do tonight. What made you not quit the team tonight?" Brady sat for a couple of seconds and then quietly spoke, "It's all I've got, Coach." "You said that at half-time," Cleveland replied, "what do you mean?" Brady sighed and stared right at Cleveland, obviously not wanting to carry the conversation any further but knowing there was no way to avoid it. After a long, awkward silence he began, "Coach, there is nothing good in my life. My dad died when I was seven in a drug deal that went bad. My mom is who knows where, probably strung out on dope. I haven't seen my mom in over two years. She will occasionally call me around a holiday or something and tell me she's going to get her life straight and come back home, but she never does. I live in my uncle's house. It's a crack house. I go to bed each night and after I go to sleep he usually has people over. They'll do their drugs and the next morning I wake up having no clue who the person is sleeping beside me. After I go to bed my uncle's friends will get high and they'll stumble into the room and sleep off the high in my room beside me. My uncle sold my bike for drugs when I was ten. Many times there is no food in the fridge. My grades are low, but high enough to play ball. Without football I really don't care if I live or die." Keith suddenly broke the silence, "Hey Coach, he ain't lying. This summer we were at some apartments and a dude got up in the back of a truck with a gun and started shooting at us. There were a bunch of us. We all took off running. Mac was there." Mac shook his head in agreement. "Coach, man," Keith continued, "I never ran so fast in my life. Then I got around the corner to look back at the guy that was shooting and there was Brady, just calmly walking off. The dude was still shooting all around." Cleveland interrupted, "Hold it, Brady. You tellin' me a guy stands up in the back of a truck with a gun, begins shooting and all your friends run but all you can do is walk off?" Brady replied, "Well, Coach, it's like I said. There ain't nothing good in my life so I ain't afraid to die. It can't get much worse. I am afraid of where I go when I die, but I'll be honest with you Coach, I ain't afraid to die." The bus was silent for several minutes then Jamie suddenly burst out as if not wanting to say anything but knowing he needed to. "What do ya mean, you're afraid of where you'll go?" Jamie asked. Brady replied, "I don't wanna go to hell. I know they say it could be worse than here. I can't imagine that, but they say it could." "Where are you goin?" Jamie asked. "I don't know. Nobody does!" Brady replied sharply. "Well I know!" Jamie shot back. "Where you goin?" Brady asked. "You going to heaven or hell?" "Heaven," Jamie said quickly. "Says who?" asked Brady. "God," Jamie answered. Brady hesitated then said, "So God came to you one night and said, 'Jamie, when you die you get to come to live with me'," Brady said in a sarcastic tone. Jamie was unphased by the sarcasm and continued, "No. The way God talks to me is through the Bible. In the Bible He says that if I admit that I do bad things and I believe that Jesus died on the cross to pay the penalty for those bad things and I accept that gift that Jesus gave by dying on a cross for us and make him Lord of my life, then I'll go to Heaven when I die. I've done all these things, so the Bible tells me I'm going to go to heaven and one day I'll see my mom again." The bus was silent for some time following that. Brady, after about five minutes, looked at Jamie and finally blurted out, "I want that!" "Want what?" Jamie asked. "You know, sins forgiven, accept Jesus, go to Heaven, all that." "Me too," McAfee spoke up quickly. Jamie said, "Well, pray." "Pray what?" Brady retorted. Jamie said, "Well, tell God what he already knows and that you are a sinner then tell Him you believe that Jesus died for your sins and that you accept his gift by dying on the cross and then you accept Jesus as your Savior." "That's all," Brady asked. "Yeah, Jamie replied. It's not hard." "But really, man, I'm not as good as you, I'm bad. I've done a lot of bad things in my life," Brady said. "God is good," Jamie replied. Brady then shot back, "Naw, man. I mean I've been really bad. You don't know the stuff I've done." "Well," Jamie replied, "God does, and I can guarantee you that His good is better than your bad is bad." Brady then turned to McAfee and asked, "You gonna do it, Mac"? "Done it," McAfee replied. Bridges is right. When I die I'll be hangin' with God. The rest of the bus ride was quiet as the fatigue from the day's activities took effect.

CHAPTER 8

The following week was a tense one for the coaches. The next opponent would be The Camden Fairview Cardinals. Camden was a team much like Lake Hamilton. The Cardinals were not going to win conference but on any given Friday night they might sneak up and bite you. What made the week more tense than normal was what had happened the previous year. One of the few wins last year was against Camden. Everything clicked on all cylinders that night for Arkansas High and Camden had a bad night. Arkansas High had built a big lead by the end of the third quarter. It helped that Camden had had several players sustain injuries during the game as well. Soon after the fourth quarter began Cleveland pulled off the first teamers to keep from running the score up and allow the other kids to play. Camden really began moving the ball down the field at that point against the second team and quickly scored. The second team offense for Arkansas High went on the field and ran three plays and had to punt. Camden again scored quickly against the second team defense and suddenly it was a game again. Cleveland became furious that the opposing coaches, who were friends of his, were taking advantage of his good will and still playing their first team while he was pulling off the dogs. The opposing coaches were just trying to win. Cleveland put the first teamers back in for Arkansas High and they quickly scored and he decided following the touchdown to kick an onside kick so that Arkansas High could recover the ball and just run the clock out with the second team offense rather than having to put the first team defense back on the field. The opposing team and fans felt that this onside kick was an attempt to run up the score and an insult to them. To make matters worse a player from the opposing team was injured on the onside kick trying to recover the ball. The game ended with an injured player being taken off the field to the hospital and the two teams refusing to shake hands after the game because of the ill-will. The two coaching staffs had previously had a very good relationship getting together at every coaches' meeting possible. Following the incident in this game there was very little communication between the two camps. The Camden newspaper had also run a couple of articles portraying Arkansas High in a very bad light, especially Coach Cleveland. One particular article stated "the lack of class that Arkansas High had was a direct reflection of their coach".

This year Arkansas High would be traveling to Camden to play. Because of the events last year school security officers would be traveling with the team to the game. Typically Arkansas High would not carry any security at all but this year was much different. Cleveland was very nervous about the whole situation. Recently there had been several letters to the editor in the Camden paper talking about the game the previous year and how disliked Cleveland was in the Camden community. Friday afternoon saw the stress at its highest level. The team was getting their equipment ready and uniforms together to load on the buses. Cleveland and most of the other coaches had gathered in Cleveland's office. The office was very quiet and tense. Often times before games there is a little bit of tension just about the ball game but it is usually still a fairly light atmosphere. This particular day there was nothing but heavy tension throughout the office. All of the coaches had some level of fear about what type of atmosphere they would walk into tonight. There was even a greater fear as to how Cleveland would react to anything said about the game so the coaches just kept quiet to ensure they didn't upset him before the game. Coach Holly suddenly broke the silence bursting into the office. He was wearing a windbreaker even though the afternoon had been quite warm. Holly spoke up and said, "Sounds like a dang morgue in here! Who died?" Cleveland looked at Holly and said, "We all might. Not much tellin' what'll happen tonight." Holly then replied, "I'll tell ya one dang thing, no matter what happens I'll be ready!" Cleveland scowled at Holly and said sarcastically, "How in the world are you gonna be prepared? You were there last year. You have seen the articles. Tell me oh wise one what do you know that has prepared you for tonight." Holly began to take off his wind breaker to reveal a t-shirt that he was wearing underneath it. As he opened the wind breaker suddenly it became clear he had some writing on his T-shirt. The letters spelled out 'Don't shoot me' across the front. Holly then turned around to reveal the back of the shirt which read 'I'm just the assistant coach', and below that was written 'Cleveland' with an arrow pointing beside it in one direction. "See," Holly said, "I just stand here on this side of you and the arrow points right at you." The coach's office went silent. The other assistant coaches were in stunned silence to wait and see if Cleveland was going to actually kill or not. At that point Cleveland began to laugh and the tension that had built over the entire week had suddenly gone.

Arkansas High arrived and much to their surprise there was nothing different than usual. No angry parents, no mob scenes, no one greeting them with signs. The game also went without much fanfare except cheers going up from the Arkansas side as the offense racked up 21 points by half-time. The defense had only given up a field goal making the game 21 to 3 at half. The coaches gathered outside the locker room and the kids waited inside. Cleveland called the staff over. "Okay guys, we have a similar scenario that is setting up this year as we did last year. How can we avoid letting what happened last year happen again?" Doc and Holly protested. Holly spoke up and said, "After last year when we let up and they tried to force the issue. I say we just keep on playing. Do you remember the fans screaming? Do you remember the newspaper articles that said our school had no class. Are you telling us that you want to let up? I say if we do that we are setting up the same scenario as last year." Doc then interjected, "Denny, when you've got a sun of a gun down you take that pocket knife out of your pocket and you finish off that sun of a gun!" Cleveland stood silently, then as if he heard nothing of the conversation said, "Okay, this is what we'll do. I'm not doing a bunch of wholesale substituting. I'll pull out some of the linemen and give McAfee a bunch of breaks. Bridges, I'm going to restrict him just to running plays. Ya'll do what you want with the defense." Cleveland looked at the coaches and smiled and said, "Yep, that's what we'll do. Thanks for your help." Then Cleveland walked into the locker room. Holly and Doc stood staring at each other. Doc then said, "You know, that son of a gun is from around these parts and feels like he is one of em." Holly replied, "Yeah, he's soft. He hasn't been around. He'll learn."

The second half saw Arkansas High put up two more touchdowns while the defense allowed a touchdown and a field goal making the outcome 35 to 13. As with each of the other games the cartons of Twinkies and Ho-Ho's rained down on the field. There were many Arkansas High fans at the game because Camden was only an hour and a half drive from Texarkana. Many of the fans had become quite used to picking up a box of snack cakes on the way to the game and bringing them. All the kids looked as forward to the snack cakes as they did to winning the ball games. George made his way over to get his customary box. Someone always made sure that George got his just reward for a game well played.

CHAPTER 9

With four regular season games left Arkansas High was now tied with Pine Bluff and El Dorado for first place in the conference. Pine Bluff would be the next opponent. Pine Bluff was ranked third in the state while El Dorado was ranked seventh. Arkansas High was not listed in the top ten. Pine Bluff, Watson Chapel and El Dorado would all play Arkansas High at Arkansas High. The final regular season game would be an away game at Sheridan. Arkansas

High had placed themselves in a position where they could control their own destiny. If they could beat Pine Bluff and El Dorado they would be in the driver's seat. Both games would be big tests. If they could win those games Watson Chapel and Sheridan should not be real difficult contests. By winning all the rest of the games that would ensure a conference championship for Arkansas High and home field advantage in the play off.

After Monday's practice Cleveland called the team over and said, "Men, you've done a good job so far this year. And I'm pleased with being undefeated in conference. That is something to be proud of. You can all look at that and be proud. But men, all you've done so far is win the games that you're supposed to. The three conference teams you've beaten are teams that you should have beaten. Two of the last four teams we play should definitely be wins. The game this week will determine if we are just another average team that wins the games that they should win, or if we plan to be contenders for a conference title. Pine Bluff will be a solid team. They are going to come out and they're gonna hit us in the mouth. But if you come out and play hard you can win this game. If you don't come out to play hard you'll be embarrassed." Cleveland looked at the team and said, "We won't be embarrassed." Keith jumped up to his feet and said, "Wolves don't get embarrassed." Then the rest of the defense stood and howled in unison with Keith. Cleveland then looked at Jamie and said, "Bridges?" Bridges looked back quietly and said, "Offense will be ready, don't worry about that." "Alright, men," Cleveland said, "Who's got me?" One of the players stood as the coaches walked off and the team began to pray. Following the prayer Jamie shouted, "First offense, let's go!" The offensive players headed back to the practice field. Cleveland was half way to the coach's office and turned to Coach Dee and said, "I gotta see what they're doing." "What, the offense?" Dee asked. "Aw, they have some silly trick plays they're working on." Cleveland walked over as they were lining up. The players all stopped what they were doing to take notice of Coach Cleveland. "Carry on," Cleveland called out. "Act like I'm not here." Jamie called out the signals and turned and handed the ball to McAfee off tackle. McAfee ran through the hole. Cleveland thought to himself,

'What was special about that? This is a play we run every week many times. They just ran it several times in practice. Why in the world would this be a special play?' He then noticed Farmer throwing the ball back to the center. Cleveland then looked at McAfee who didn't have the ball. Cleveland looked stunned as the kids moved back to the line of scrimmage. Cleveland said, "Run it again." The players lined up again and again Jamie turned to hand the ball to McAfee. Cleveland noticed that Jamie didn't have the ball in his hand that he put in McAfee's mid-section. As he continued to watch he noticed Farmer not moving, still hunched over in the backfield as if ready to pass block. Suddenly Farmer took off with the ball. Cleveland then moved from the sideline to behind the offense. "Okay, run it again," Cleveland said. From the vantage point behind the players he could see that Jamie put the ball behind his back as he turned to fake the hand-off to McAfee. His left hand was put in McAfee's stomach faking the hand-off while his right hand held the ball behind his back. As he went back to hand off to McAfee Farmer took a half step to the left to get out of Jamie's way and the ball was slipped into Farmer's mid-section from behind Jamie's back. McAfee doubled over as if getting the handoff from Jamie and carried out the fake. Jamie then rolled right away from Farmer faking a roll-out pass. Farmer hesitated as if he were pass blocking until the defense had shifted away from him. The ball was tucked in his belly and when the area cleared he took off running. Cleveland stood with his mouth gaping open. "Where did this play come from?" McAfee spoke up and said, "This is the quarterback special or game breaker." Cleveland then looked at Jamie, "Bridges, where did you see this run?" "I didn't Coach," Jamie replied, "I just thought about it and figured it would work." "Hmm," Cleveland said. He looked around and said, "Yeah, I like it. I like it. You don't risk much, I mean, yeah, a blind hand-off but that's not real risky. And you can practice the technique to get the hand-off right. The linemen will never see the handoff and the linebackers are going to key on McAfee because he's going to be the first thing out of the backfield. If they don't fall for the fake they're going to think Jamie has the roll out and that may freeze the d-backs as well. Then BOOM! outta nowhere, Farmer breaks for it! I like it, but don't run it unless we're in a bad bind. I don't wanna show this until we have to. Carry on, men!" With that Cleveland walked back to the coach's office while the offense spent a little more time perfecting the quarter back special, as they called it.

As Cleveland moved back into the coach's office he was greeted by Coach Files. "Denny, do you mind if I do the pre-game talk with the kids this week. It's a big game and I'd be honored if I could do it." Cleveland hesitated a minute and said, "Yeah, yeah, I guess that would be fine. You know that is not exactly my favorite task. I know the head coach usually does the pre-game talk, but I just figure by game day the hay is in the barn and if they're not ready to play by Friday night a little 5 minute talk is not gonna do a whole lot. So yeah, yeah, Files. That'll be just fine." Then Cleveland hesitated and looked back at him and said, "Just one thing, though. I know you like the dramatic, Files but let's not get crazy with this, okay?" "Oh, no! Coach Cleveland," Files replied, "this is way to big of a game to do something crazy. I'll have 'em ready, I'll have 'em fired up, but there won't be anything crazy. It'll just be a good ole talkin' to." "Alright," Cleveland said then walked off.

Friday night arrived with much fanfare. Pine Bluff made their presence known even before the game started. Pine Bluff had one of the largest bands in the state and their percussion section was just a slight step down from Grambling. When they walked into the stadium everyone knew it. There was an energy about the band that no other band in the state could replicate. The band emerged through the gates of the stadium and only the percussion section was playing. The echoes of the drums pounded off the old concrete stadium suddenly giving a new intensity to the game's atmosphere. The band made a full lap around the track before entering the stands. Even the Arkansas High fans had a new energy with the Pine Bluff band walking through. They moved with precision moved back to their side of the stadium and eased up into the bleachers without missing a single beat the percussion section continued to play. Once the band was completely in place they stood for a count of five and suddenly the percussion stopped and the band all sat down in unison. Suddenly the stadium was deafeningly quiet. The players finished their warm ups before the game and made their way to the locker room. The locker room was quiet when Coach Files and the rest of the coaches walked into the room. The other coaches kind of stood at the back of the room and Coach Files stepped forward to address the players. "Men, this is the biggest game you've played in your whole lives. We have a chance to beat the number three team in the state. Men, those guys have two of the best athletes I've ever seen. There has not been a team this entire year that has been able to stop their running back and there has not been an offense this year that has been able to run over their middle linebacker. But men, do you know why we'll beat them? We'll beat them because a good team playing together will always beat a great player playing alone. They have two great players who play alone. We have eleven men on each side of the ball who play together." Coach Files then moved across the room and picked up a bag. At that moment Doc and Coach Holly walked into the dressing room beside Cleveland. Cleveland whispered to him as Files picked up the bag and began to open it, "Oh, my dear heavens. He has a bag." Holly whispered less loudly than Cleveland, "What's in the bag?" Files moved back to the front of the room and said, "Men, I found this in my yard today." Coach Files pulled a dead chicken out of the sack. "Oh, my." Cleveland sighed. Holly, knowing that Cleveland was bothered by this turn in the pre-game talk, decided to add a little more to Cleveland's uneasiness. "Hey, David, David!" he whispered loudly. "Did you tell Files to shake a dead chicken at the boys to get 'em fired up tonight? I've seen a lot of pre-game talks and I can guarantee you no other coach that I've ever seen, or nothing they've ever done involved shaking a dead chicken at a team!" "Men," Files continued, "this chicken got away from the rest of the chickens. All the chickens were walking around the yard together. But suddenly this chicken decided not to be a team player. He wanted to be the big chicken. And you know what happened?" Files paused to give an element of the dramatic. He held the chicken up and walked through the players as he paused, "An animal," he continued, "an animal killed him! I don't know what kind of animal it was. But you know why he got killed? He got away from the team." Suddenly one of the defensive players stood and shouted, "A wolf killed the chicken!" and then he howled. The rest of the team howled back in unison. Keith jumped to his feet and screamed, "Be the wolf!" The rest of the team howled and then some shouted, "Kill the chicken!" Files began to try to regain control of the players and calm the team down. He tried to redirect their thoughts back to the point that he was trying to make which was, that they should play as a team. It was no use they continued to chant "Kill the chicken! Kill the chicken!" and then they would howl. Files, at a loss, looked toward Cleveland. Cleveland waited a moment, then walked to the front of the team and shouted, "Now let's not just talk about it! Let's get out there and kill the chicken!" The team tore out of the locker room onto the side line and jumped and chanted as they began to get ready to run through the run-through sign. They were all hollering, "Kill the chicken! Kill the chicken! Be the wolf! Be the wolf!"

Back in the locker room Files stood dejected, wondering what had happened. His talk had started out so well, he had a nice visual, and he was headed right to his point and then he suddenly lost 'em. Shaking his head, not knowing what to say, Coach Holley walked over to him and said, "Files, Pine Bluff's mascot is a zebra, not a chicken." Files just shook his head then walked out on the field with the rest of the team. Holly and Doc made their way to the door. Holly stopped and looked at Cleveland and said, "Coach, and we're supposed to beat the number three team in the state with a bunch of yahoos like that?" Cleveland shook his head and started to walk out to the field. Holly walked behind him. "Coach, you know we're probably going to get some calls about that chicken shaking incident." Cleveland shook his head and just continued to walk away. Doc then turned to Holly and said, "I was afraid he was going to put some voodoo curse on somebody with that chicken."

Pine Bluff received the opening kick-off and immediately was shut down on three successive plays. Each play ended with a scream by the defense of "Kill the chicken!" and a howl from the entire defense. Pine Bluff punted to Arkansas High. On the opening play Jamie changed the play from the typical running play that they almost always started each game with. He decided to test the defense with a deep pass over the middle to Knight. He dropped back and quickly spotted Knight over the middle. Knight was able to break free and finally was dragged down at the Pine Bluff 20 yard line. Three plays later McAfee had punched the ball into the end zone putting Arkansas High up 7 to 0. By half time Arkansas High was ahead 14 to 7. Toward the end of the third quarter Pine Bluff began to pound their big running back at the tired Arkansas High defense. The Zebras scored to even up the game 14 to 14. When Arkansas High got the ball back they slowly moved down their field and from the 1 yard line Kyle Farmer punched the ball across for a touchdown making the score 21 to 14 in favor of Arkansas High. With 2 minutes remaining in the game the score was still Arkansas High 21 and Pine Bluff 14. The defense had the Zebras 3rd and 8 on the Zebras 40 yard line. Pine Bluff called a time out and Arkansas High players came to the sideline. Doc walked out into the middle of the players and said, "This is where you test your heart. Stop these son of a guns on the next two plays and the game is ours. Look men, be ready for anything. They're getting desperate. Get back out there men! Two plays! That's all we gotta do is two plays, stop 'em twice." The teams ran back out onto the field and lined up. Pine bluff snapped the ball and handed off to the big back who broke a tackle at the line and broke into the secondary. He was slowed trying to evade the free safety, giving Brady a chance to catch up from behind. Running as hard as he could Brady was able to grab a piece of his jersey but the big back drug Brady a few yards and then shook loose and then sprinted in for a touchdown. After the touchdown Pine Bluff went for a two point conversion and blasted the big back in for a successful two point conversion making the score 22 to 21 in favor of Pine Bluff. Jamie and the rest of the offense went back on the field. Arkansas High had the ball on their own 20 with one time out left and 80 yards to go. Jamie took the snap and rolled left. He spotted Knight in the flats and threw the ball toward him. The ball hit him in the hands and then bounced away for an incomplete pass. Jamie was hit after the throw and walked over to the official as if to complain about being hit late. "Hey, Mr. Referee!" he hollered, "did you see that?" As Jamie made his way closer he said, "Sir, we have a special play. Please don't blow the whistle until you see the ball either on the ground or in the end zone. It's a little deceptive. The full back is going to get the ball." Jamie then began to walk away from the official saying loudly "Keep an eye on those guys they are hitting late." One of the offensive receivers came in to replace Knight bringing a play from the side line. He ran into the huddle but Jamie said, "Okay, guys. gamebreaker. We've got it down. Our backs are against the wall. If we do it just like we've practiced we'll pull out a win here. Okay? We've done it enough, we know what to do." The offense lined up.

The crowd was quiet. The Arkansas High crowd could almost sense the game was slipping away. Jamie took the snap, moved to his right, slipped the ball into Farmer's belly while at the same time faking the handoff to McAfee. Jamie then rolled out. The defense was looking more for a pass knowing that time was about to expire and when Jamie rolled out they bit hook, line and sinker rolling with him. Farmer waited what seemed to be an eternity and then looked and saw no one in front of him. He tucked the ball into his left arm and began to move down the field. He broke into a full sprint before anyone noticed and by the time they realized he had the ball it was too late. He was off to the races and scored. The game was now 27 to 22. Arkansas High then went for 2 to make sure there was a 7 point spread between the two. They handed the ball off to McAfee who bounced into the end zone making the score 29 to 22. Pine Bluff walked to the side lines stunned, still not knowing how in the world the full back had gotten the ball and scored on them. They had them stopped.

Arkansas High then lined up to kick the ball off. Pine Bluff was unable to move the ball after the kick off and the clock ran out. Word had spread each week about George's Twinkies and Ho-Ho's. Coach Dee's wife brought her usual box of snack cakes down for George but so did many other people who threw them down on the track for the rest of the kids. The players celebrated as sugary snacks rained down onto the track. Several of the players went over to the track and picked up a box or two and finally all the boxes were picked up. There were over 30 boxes thrown out onto the track for the players. More fans seemed to notice indicating that probably next week there might even be more. It had become an event with the fans to celebrate a victory by throwing snack cakes down on the field for the players. Most of the fans really had no idea why in the world they were doing it, but it was fun and it was their own special way of helping out the team. The players moved into the locker room. It was filled with singing, celebrating and howling. The defense was hollering "We killed the chicken! We killed the chicken! We're the wolves!" Cleveland walked in. "Men, this is a great win. This is one of the best wins I've been around. Men, you've proven that you want to be a contender this year. You've proven that you want to fight for a conference title. You've gone above and beyond being the team that just wins the games they were supposed to. I'll be honest with you, men. We weren't supposed to win this game, but I knew deep down if you played together you would, and you did. Enjoy the weekend. Celebrate this win all weekend, because Monday it's back to work."

Next Monday Cleveland was in his office enjoying what would probably be a pretty easy prep week. Watson Chapel was the next team on the schedule and they were the worst team in the conference this year. The phone rang and Lisa called over the intercom, "Coach Cleveland, Dr. Carr is on line one." Cleveland answered and then he heard, "Coach, congratulations! I have not ever enjoyed a game as much as I did that one last Friday night. I heard a couple of people around me saying it looked like the good ole state championship days." Cleveland replied, "It was a good win alright but I don't know if I'd go so far as state championship and all that." Carr then butted in, "Denny, don't sell the victory short. I can't recall a bigger win since I've been with the district. This win will start bringing the fans back. I tell ya Denny, the cafeteria food still stinks, but you're doing your job." "Well, thank you," Cleveland replied. Carr began again, "Denny, I've had several calls about kicking a dead chicken around in the pre-game talk. Normally I'd be very upset about something of that magnitude, but Denny, sometimes it takes drastic measures to wake up a team. I understand that you're just trying to wake up the boys and get 'em ready to play. However I cannot conceive of how kicking a dead chicken gets a team fired up to beat a team called the Zebras. Denny, ya'll didn't put black and white strips on that chicken, did ya?" Before Denny could respond Carr interrupted, "Well, that's your business, Denny. I'll stay out of your business as long as you make my life easy. But Denny, in a few weeks we'll play the El Dorado Wildcats. Don't ya'll go and kill somebody's pet cat and kick it around the locker room, alright? Can you promise me that? Well, Denny, I gotta go. Keep up the good work." Carr then hung up the phone.

Watson Chapel arrived at Arkansas High. The team and cheerleaders were about the only ones who made the trip. It is about a three hour drive from Watson Chapel. A handful of parents dotted the visitors side. The home stands were almost as full as they were against Pine Bluff. Cleveland looked at the crowd and thought, 'maybe Carr was right about the renewed interest as a result of the Pine Bluff win.' Dee walked up and said, "Hey, Coach. It's cool to win in front of a big crowd, isn't it?" Holly stepped up and interjected before Cleveland could speak, "Just more people to run us out of town on a rail if we get by this bunch of yahoos." Cleveland turned to Holly and said, "We won't get beat by this group. We could play our second team and we wouldn't get beat by this group."

The game started with three long sustained drives by Arkansas High resulting in three touchdowns. By half time the score was 28 to 0 Arkansas High. Much of the second half was played by players who never see much action during the year. The game ended in a lopsided victory for Arkansas High of 42 to 14. Again, the Hostess boxes which seemed like 20 or 30 the week before were closer to 40 or 50 this week. Snack cakes were being handed over the rail and thrown down onto the track. The younger players who had finally seen action in their first real game of the season were gobbling up the boxes as quickly as they could be thrown. George was actually able to enjoy the entire fourth quarter from the bench eating on snack cakes. Coach Dee's wife, had brought George his box of snack cakes once the game was out of hand.

Chapter 10

The following week Arkansas High would play El Dorado at home. El Dorado and Arkansas High were the only two unbeaten teams left in conference. El Dorado had now moved up to #2 in the state rankings, while Arkansas High was ranked 6th. Monday's practice was spent working on the weaknesses the coaches had seen on film the day before. After practice Coach Files approached Cleveland. "Coach, got another big game this week. This week do you mind if I do the pre-game talk?" Cleveland stood in stunned silence. After the dead chicken fiasco he figured there would be no way Files would ever ask to give a pre-game talk again. Files continued, "I got the boys goin', didn't I, for the Pine Bluff game, ya know?" Cleveland shook his head and took a deep sigh. Files then said, "Coach, we won that game. And you know the boys have never come out as fired up as they did in that first quarter against Pine Bluff." Cleveland then looked Files in the eye and said, "Files, you shook a dead chicken at the kids. After you shook a dead chicken at the kids, they had no clue what point you were trying to get across. They then totally missed your point and in spite of all that still won. Then the following week I get a call from the superintendent because parents called him saying that you shook a dead chicken at 'em. And you want to do another pre-game talk?" "But Coach,:" Files replied, "the kids played like wild men. You have to admit that." "But they had no idea why!" Cleveland shot back. "But do they ever?" Files asked. There was silence. Then Files said, "Coach, we won." Cleveland took a long pause, "Yeah, yeah, you're right. We won." Cleveland looked around a minute and said, "Yeah, you're probably right. I don't know that they know what I'm talking about half the time. Yeah, okay. Yeah, you can do it. Just Files, no crazy stuff, okay? And that includes dead animals, okay?" "You got it Coach."

As the week progressed so did the hype surrounding the game. The state newspaper touted this week's game between El Dorado and Arkansas High as the game of the week. The ticket office also saw a dramatic rise in ticket sales. This week's game attendance would be close to the number of fans who watched the Texas High game. The coaches tried to keep the focus on winning the conference title. The conference champion would play at home throughout the play-offs until the final state championship game which would be held in Little Rock. Even though both teams still had one game remaining after this match up, the winner of this game would be conference champion. If the winner of this week lost, next week it would make the conference record equal which would then revert to a tie-breaker of head to head games. The tie breaker would still make the winner of this game the conference champion. Friday night finally arrived. The hype surrounding the game made the week seem to pass much more slowly than the other weeks. It was a cool, damp night. It had rained the morning of the game. The kids sat quietly in the locker room before the game. Coach Files walked into the locker room followed by the rest of the coaching staff. Holly saw this as an opportunity to make his way over to Cleveland and possibly whisper some encouragement to Cleveland while Files gave his pre-game talk. Holly walked over to Cleveland and whispered, "Hope Files didn't drive to school the way I did this morning." Cleveland turned looking inquisitively, almost afraid to ask, "Why not?" "Well," Holly said with a big sigh, "there was a big armadillo that had been hit by a truck. I figured Files, if he had seen it, would pick it up and paint it purple and pass it off as an El Dorado panther, since El Dorado's mascot is the panther. Although it doesn't seem to matter to him what mascot it is, he just seems to like to shake dead animals." Cleveland looked at Holly and said, "He promised no dead animals this week."

Files began speaking, "Men, we are a team and a team works together. My Bible in the book of Ecclesiastes says that two men are better than one because if one falls the other one can help him up, and that two working together can do much more work than they can separately. Men, have you seen geese fly?" A few players kind of shook their head as if they had. "Bridges," Files continued, "what's different about how the geese fly?" "Well Coach," Bridges replied, "they form kind of a V pattern." "That's exactly right!" Files screamed. "They fly in a V, 'cause if they're in a V they are more aerodynamic and that means the wind resistance is less. If the wind resistance is less it's easier for them to fly because they're working together. They can fly further and faster if they fly in formation. The birds are drafting off of each other. If they do this they get a lot more accomplished. Men, if we play as a team we will go much further in this season. But if we don't work together, if we play as individuals, we'll fail. So tonight, we're gonna run on the field in V formation to symbolize that we're working together as a team." Holly immediately turned to Cleveland, "This oughta be good for a chuckle." Cleveland looked back and said, "Well, at least there are no dead animals." Files continued with his pre-game talk and finally as he got to the end he said, "Now men. Let's go out there and let's form that V and work together as a team." The players ran out of the locker room and got behind the run through sign the cheerleaders had made. The players stood there trying to figure out how in the world they would form a V and run onto the field. The El Dorado team had lined up behind their sign and run through it and had gotten to the sideline. The cheerleaders always would do a particular cheer known as 'calling the hogs' just before the players would run onto the field. The cheerleaders had now called the hogs three times. The players were still behind the sign trying to determine who would like up where in the V. An official walked over to warn the coaches that they needed to get their players on the field or they would be charged with a delay of game penalty. Finally Coach Hollinshead who had already made his way onto the sideline with the rest of the coaches walked back over to the players and screamed, "Now get out there, now!" The players jumped and were startled and began running through the sign in what they attempted to make look like a V but definitely gave no semblance and no one in the stands could determine what in the world they were doing. It was just a group of young men running while holding hands. Hollingshead looked at Cleveland and said, "If they were only running through a flower covered field it would make a nice Hallmark Card."

The game started and the first series saw El Dorado on offense start from their own 20 yard line. The first two plays were running plays which went for very small gains and on 3rd and 8 the El Dorado quarterback dropped back to pass. Keith broke through the line, stripped the ball from the quarterback as he sacked him. The ball was rolling free and Blake Brady scooped it up and ran in for a touchdown. Keith immediately jumped up and followed Brady into the end zone and they celebrated by flapping their wings and shouting "we are the birds". By the end of the first half the score was 14 to 0 with Arkansas High leading. The defense, led by Keith howling a flapping their arms every time they made a big defensive stop, which had been many in the first half as they completely shut down El Dorado.

As the players entered the locker room for half time the score was now 14 to 0. The defense was led by Keith flapping his wings and howling. Cleveland stood in front of the players, quietened them down and said, "Men, we've got 'em shell shocked. Those guys, and the rest of the state for that matter, thought they would just come in here and you would roll over for 'em." Cleveland looked over at Keith and said, "Keith, when you stripped that ball and Brady picked it up and scored that sent them reeling. They never recovered. They didn't know how to react. Men, they are used to winning. El Dorado has been ahead the entire game in most of their previous games. When they found themselves suddenly down they had no clue. They couldn't react. Men, this is a good team we're playing out there though. And they will get their bearings. They'll get their feet back under them. They are going to be ready for you the second half. They are going to come out with fire and intensity and if you come out flat, if you come out thinking you've got this game won you will be beaten badly. Men, you can't let them up for air. You've got to kick 'em while they're down. 'Cause I'm tellin' ya, this team can get back in this game very quickly." The players and coaches broke into their sub-groups, offense going to one part of the dressing room and the defense going to another part of the dressing room to go over some adjustments that needed to be made. The adjustments on defense were very few. The defense had come out and the game plan had worked splendidly. Offensively there were just a few minor changes. But in both sub-groups the coaches emphasized 'if you let 'em back into the game they will beat you'.

The players headed back onto the field for the second half. The second half started with Arkansas High receiving the kick off. The kick landed in Knight's arms and he was able to run the ball back up to the 30 yard line. Jamie walked into the huddle and called a play. The team approached the line of scrimmage. The first play was a hand-off left tackle to McAfee. He picked up about 4 yards. The next play was another hand-off to McAfee except this time on the right side of the line. After McAfee picked up 4 more yards Cleveland turned to the coaches and said, "That's it. We just keep pounding the ball at McAfee until they stop him and then we figure out what to do after that. The more we run the ball the more we run the clock, maybe we can get this game over with quick." It was now 3rd down and 2 yards to go. Arkansas High was on their own 38 yard line. The play came into the huddle from the sideline.

Cleveland had called another running play to McAfee over the left tackle. Jamie, knowing that everyone including El Dorado, was expecting them just to continue to run to McAfee until El Dorado stopped them changed the play in the huddle. Jamie looked over and said, "McAfee, I'm gonna fake the hand-off to you then I'm heading around the right end. I want you to give me a good fake." Jamie took the snap and he turned and faked the hand-off to McAfee and it was if the entire El Dorado defense moved in to stop him, determined to keep him from picking up the 1st down. Jamie trotted around the right end as if carrying out the rest of the fake. As Jamie moved toward the end of the line and turned the corner he took off into open field. The fake had been carried out perfectly and by the time the defensive backs were able to react to what was happening it was too late. Jamie raced down the field and into the end zone. The score was suddenly 21 to 0 and the Arkansas High side of the stadium roared while the El Dorado players, coaches and fans stood in stunned silence. It was as if what little bit of wind that was in El Dorado's sail was coming out after half time was suddenly deflated. Sometimes in football games the players are still physically out there on the field but no longer mentally. This is what happened with El Dorado as soon as Jamie stepped across that goal line. El Dorado was still physically on the field, but mentally it seemed as if they were somewhere else.

Jamie was greeted with high fives and pats on the back as he reached the sideline. The game ended with Arkansas High winning 28 to 14. Arkansas High was able to build their lead to 28 to 0 and was able to put in the second and third teamers. El Dorado scored twice in the closing minutes of the game against the second and third team to make the game seem closer than it really was. The final gun went off and it was if realization had suddenly hit. Not only for the fans but the players as well, suddenly they were conference champions, and a team who could be considered as one of the best in the state. As the players moved to the center of the field to shake hands the fans began to exit the stadium. As the fans exited, as they made their way toward the railing, they dropped their boxes of Twinkies and Cup-cakes down onto the track. In the early weeks the number of boxes would slowly grow week by week, but as the play-off loomed closer it was if the number of boxes multiplied every week now. There were more Twinkies and Cup-cakes than George and everyone else on the team could eat. George gathered up his box, gave other boxes to some of the other players and tried to divvy out all that he could to his teammates.

The players made their way into the locker room with shouts and whoops going up from the players as they entered. Keith and Brady were comparing plays. Keith shouted, "Brady, aw man! I busted that quarterback. I heard him grunt when I hit him! Aw, man, and then that ball came rolling out and I wanted so bad to get it and I looked up and there you were. You were scooping up that ball and headed for the end zone. Man! Man, Brady, I thought 'this is the best day of my life'!" "Your life?" Brady said, "What about me? I got up this morning next to some doped up junkie, but you know what? I left that nasty house that had nothing in the fridge for breakfast. And you know what, Keith? I knew. I just knew it. I knew God was going to give me a good day today. When I hit that end zone with the ball, I thought 'God, if heaven's better than this, that's got to be an awesome place.' I've never felt so good in my life!"

Cleveland burst into the room and suddenly the room was quiet. Cleveland looked at the players and stood in silence. Keith spoke up, "What's up Coach?" Cleveland took a breath and hesitated, looked around, and after a long silence finally said, "I am standing in front of the conference champions!" Some of the players responded with, "Yeah, yeah." Cleveland continued again, "I mean, I mean, ya'll are conference champions! Men, you know what this feels like? Sometimes they talk about people climbing a mountain, and they talk about how foggy it is. And they say that those people just keep climbing and climbing. They can't see where they're going and they don't know how far they've got to go, and then suddenly it's as if the fog clears, and they look up and there's no more mountain to climb. They're at the top. They can look out over all of God's creation. Men, as far as the conference is concerned, we've done that! We've reached the top! Now we can look around and see the year that's behind us. Men, it's as if the fog cleared tonight, and here we are. We're on top. Now men, that doesn't mean we're through. This is great and we're going to have a good weekend celebrating this. But men, do you know what you do when you finish climbing one mountain?" Several of the players responded with "No, no. What do you do, Coach?" "When you climb one mountain the next thing you do," said Cleveland, "is find a bigger mountain. So, men, next week let's take care of business against Sheridan then let's climb the biggest mountain that's out there. Let's climb the State Championship Mountain." Roars went up from the players as they jumped up and shouted and celebrated.

Chapter 11

The final regular season game of the year would be against the Sheridan Yellow Jackets. Sheridan's only win thus far this year in conference was against Watson Chapel and that game was a struggle. Cleveland had received a call Friday night immediately after the El Dorado game. The call was from the head coach at Sheridan. "Denny," he said, "What do you think about moving our game from Friday night to Thursday night?" Cleveland paused a minute and said, "Well, on one hand I hate take the kids out of their routine right before the play-offs, but I wouldn't mind going and scouting a game kind of to prepare for the play-offs, and send some of the other coaches to scout other games of teams we might face." The Sheridan coach then responded, "Coach, our season has been over since October. The kids are ready to put this season to rest and Saturday is the first day of deer season. Me and most of the coaches here would love to go to the woods on Friday night and get in our deer camp and get set for Saturday. "Well," Cleveland said, "I'll probably regret it later, but yeah, let's go ahead. Let's switch it to Thursday night. You can go ahead and make whatever arrangements are necessary."

The short week's preparation was light. The players worked on core basic plays making sure they still understood their assignments on each play. The coaches spent much as much time trying to decide what games to scout on Friday night and what teams to prepare for in the play-offs as they did preparing for Sheridan.

Thursday at noon the players gathered and began loading the equipment. They put their uniforms in mesh type bags along with their shoulder pads, helmets. Each player took their mesh bag and piled it onto the back of an equipment bus. The team would be wearing their road whites, white pants and white jerseys with red numbers on it this week, since they were playing an away game. After the players had loaded equipment and uniforms the managers began loading bags of footballs, kicking tees, tape, medical bags and jugs of Gatorade. This week had been unseasonably warm for this time of year, so extra Gatorade was packed for half time of the game.

Since this was a Thursday Night away game and the athletic department was trying to save money for the playoff run, the coaches decided to take only the players who were completely necessary. Fewer players would mean they didn't have to feed as many kids during the trip and they wouldn't take as many buses. Coach Files drove one bus with Doc managing the players. Dee Holly and Cleveland rode on the other bus with the remaining players and the equipment. As Dee began pulling the equipment bus out of the parking lot instead of going through a drive he partially went over a curb which caused the bus to bounce. The jugs and the equipment shifted and made quite a racket. Holly, who sitting directly behind Dee tapped him on the shoulder and said, "Dee, let's not drive like a bloomin' idiot this week." Dee, who prided himself on his ability to not only drive a bus but be one of the few coaches who could back a bus in and out of very tight quarters, responded to Holly, "Don't worry about me, I could navigate this bus through a pile up at Daytona." "Look, Jeff Gordon," Holly shot back knowing Dee could not stand Jeff Gordon, "I just want to get to this game and get home without being killed or arrested." Dee shot back, "You just worry about the game. I'll get us there." The first half of the bus trip would be over Interstate and then the next hour and a half would be over small winding roads through little towns in Arkansas. After exiting the Interstate and moving onto one of the smaller highways Dee approached a traffic light turning from yellow to red and quickly stopped. Holly looked up from his newspaper and said, "Keep it calm, Jeff Gordon." Holly then looked down and noticed something wet running along the flooring just past his feet. The light then turned red and Dee accelerated. The liquid then ran back toward the back of the bus. Holly reached his finger down and touched the liquid thinking maybe the air conditioner was leaking in the back of the bus. When he examined the liquid he realized it had a reddish tint to it. "Who packed the Gatorade?" Holly asked. "That would be me," responded Dee. "You're also the one driving the bus like an idiot, aren't you? So that's strike one." Cleveland looked at Holly and said, "Coach, what in the world are you talking about?" "Well, it seems Jeff Gordon packed the Gatorade but didn't tape the lids down, then Jeff threw the jugs around getting us out of the parking lot at the school. The equipment including white jerseys are now soaking in red Gatorade." Dee looked back and said, "What are you talking about?" At this point they were driving through a small town. The small town had very narrow streets and utility poles were right next to the street. "Put on your brakes!" Holly barked back. Dee looked up in the rear view mirror to make sure there was no traffic behind him on the little street and then he began to apply the brakes. When he applied the brakes with a little punch the Gatorade began to run up toward the front of the bus again out from under the equipment and uniforms. Dee looked down on the floor and he could see the liquid moving toward the front of the bus from the momentum of his braking. Holly then shouted, "I'm only going to give you one strike. Even though you deserve two, you messed up twice. You didn't tape the lids and then you drove like an idiot. I just hope the uniforms aren't soaking in the Gatorade. Maybe the kids packed them on top." Cleveland was looking down shaking his head as the Gatorade ran back and forth across the floor. Suddenly Holly shouted, "Look out!" Dee looked up just in time to see that he was swerving slightly off the little highway running through the city. He quickly turned the steering wheel but not before there was a sound of a loud smash. The side view mirror on the passenger side was no longer on the bus. It was laying in the street having hit a utility pole and been smashed to bits. Cleveland jumped to attention and quickly shouted "What was that?" "A bird!" Dee shot back. "A bird? How could a bird hit tat hard?" Cleveland questioned. "It was a big dang bird." Dee replied. Suddenly Holly said, "Where's Files?" "Well behind us I would guess," replied Cleveland. "Hey kids y'all see the other bus back there?" One of the kids in the back replied, "I can see the bus but it is way back there." "Good" replied Holly. He then continued, "Dee give me that CB." The buses were equipped with CB's so that the drivers could communicate with each other in case of an emergency or breakdown. "What do you want the CB for?" asked Dee. "I gotta radio the crew chief Gordo. Just give me the dang CB." Dee reluctantly handed the CB to Holly. "Breaker 1-9, Coach Files this is Coach Holly, do you read me?" Holly shouted into the CB. "This is Coach Files and I read you loud and clear come back." "Hey Files," continued Holly, "Dee just pulverized one of the biggest birds I have ever seen. If you see his dead carcass on the road, just leave it there. I don't want no blood soaked fowl involved in our pregame speech." Files sat silently for a few seconds then replied, "10-4 the only thing we've seen in the road is a bunch of glass. Someone must have had an accident earlier." Holly and Files signed off on the CB's and Cleveland moved to the back of the bus and to begin inspecting the uniforms. The bus continued to narrowly move down the road without a passenger side mirror. Holly leaned up to Dee and whispered, "Drive on, Jeff Gordon! Drive on!" "Shut up," Dee said angrily. Holly again leaned forward and whispered in Dee's ear, "Dee, that's strike two." Dee turned around, "Look old man, if you hadn't gotten me all distracted that would have never happened." "Oh, I'm sorry, Jeff Gordon. I won't mention to you later on if let's say, something like the 'you didn't close the latch on the back door and all of our equipment falls out' or something like that. Jeff, you did secure the latch on the back door, didn't you?" "Shut up!" Dee responded.

The team bus with the equipment was the first to arrive in Sheridan. There was a small fenced in area right next to the locker rooms where all the buses would park. The equipment bus would be the first on to park in that area and they would park as close as they could to the locker room so that it would be a very short distance the kids had to carry the equipment from the bus into the locker room. As Dee pulled up he turned the bus so he could begin backing in. Since the equipment was easier to load and unload from the back of the bus this would make it very easy for the kids to unload. The bus was parked and unloaded. Once the bus was empty Dee would back it up against a space next to the fence. Dee began backing in. The space was just barely wide enough for two buses and he knew he would need to be in tight on one side so that the player bus could get beside him. Holly called out, "Hey Gordo, leave enough space for the bus to park beside us!" Dee responded, "I know, I know. I don't need your help." Cleveland had made his way back up to the front and said, "Hey where is our side mirror." "Never had one." Dee quickly shot back and kept backing in the bus. "Now I don't remember getting a bus that had no passenger side mirror." "Not easy to drive without that side mirror but I have managed," Reported Dee as he focused his attention on backing into the parking area. Just in front of the back fence there was a utility pole. Holly said, "Dee, do you want me to get off the bus and direct you in? I can give you signals where to go and what not." "Not necessary," Dee responded. Dee continued to back and turn the bus into the place. He was eyeing the fence beside him making sure that he stayed as close as he could so that he left enough room for the other bus to pull in beside him. He kept easing back then suddenly there was a big thud throughout the bus. After this thud there was a sound that resembled a sonic boom from behind the bus. "What was that?" Cleveland screamed. "I guess you could say that Jeff Gordon took the pole," Holly responded. "He not only took the pole, but my guess is from the sound that I just heard is he took out the transformer that sits on the pole." Although it was still light the stadium lights had already been turned on but after Dee hit the pole those lights went out as did the lights on the scoreboard. Dee leaned forward on the steering wheel putting his head down. "Well, Gordo, that's strike three," Holly called from behind him. The lights in the stores and fast food restaurants had been extinguished with one bump. Cleveland walked up, surveyed the scene. One of the managers looked over at Coach Cleveland as he walked up, "Hey, Coach Cleveland, it was really cool when Dee hit that pole and the transformer thing blew up." Cleveland looked at the pole and the transformer then quickly walked over to the coaches and asked, "How could this have happened?" Holly quickly responded, "I didn't get back there and direct Dee in like I should have. He ended up bumping the pole and transformer blew. He didn't hit the pole hard, it just must have shaken it. We don't have to hurry through warm-ups though. I figure it'll take 'em a couple of hours to get the lights back on." Coach Files had walked up by this times. He looked at Cleveland and said, "Hey Coach Cleveland, speaking of warm-ups. Do you mind if I give the pre-game talk?" Cleveland hesitated and then said, "Let's see. The first week you shook a dead chicken at the kids and they chanted 'kill the chicken' when they were playing the zebras. Last week the kids flapped their arms like birds when we're the Razorbacks." Files quickly interjected, "Coach, we won though, didn't we? And the kids, well they had that fire in their eye, didn't they?" Cleveland stood a moment and said, "I don't know what more damage you can do. Sure, go ahead. Just don't do anything that will get the superintendent calling me again."

The players began putting on their uniforms and they noticed as they were putting them on that the pants and jerseys were wet and pink. The white jerseys had been soaking in fruit punch flavored Gatorade for most of the trip up. The white mixing with the red of the Gatorade gave it a nice pink color. McAfee walked up to Cleveland, "Hey Coach. I don't know about this." "About what," Cleveland quickly responded. "Coach, I don't look good in pink. It ain't manly." Then Cleveland questioned, "how many of the jerseys are pink?" "Coach, almost all of them are pink." "Aw, no. Aw, no. This can't be happening!" Cleveland responded. "Okay, okay. Let's do this. Let's go wash 'em out. Go see what you can do about washing them out. McAfee then said, "Coach, this is washed out. I've already tried." Cleveland then looked at McAfee and said, "Well, just wear it. That's all we've got. We can't go back and get any others."

A large crowd was piling into the stadium. It was senior night at Sheridan. A lot of the parents of the senior athletes and senior band members and cheerleads and drill team had gathered to recognize the students. Texarkana had also brought a good crowd. Since the team now was definitely a state contender there was a lot of excitement surrounding the team. There was a good deal of interest not only from those with kids directly affected by the school, but also there was interest from other schools because of the possibility of playing against Arkansas High in play off games. Several coaches had made it over to scout the game since they were playing on Friday night and Arkansas High would be playing on Thursday night. Both teams warmed up in the dark stadium while the electricians worked furiously to fix the transformer and get the lights back on. Both coaching staffs were told that the lights should be on between 7:45 and 8:00. The start time for the game would be pushed back to 8:00. After the warm up time both teams headed for the locker room. The pink Texarkana jerseys had gone unnoticed in the dark.

Coach Files entered the locker room with his usual pre-game fire in his eye. He stood up and again began talking about playing as a team. Although he had failed to get his message across in the previous 2 pre-game talk he was bound and determined to make sure that the players understood that he wanted them to play as a team. He felt this was important going into the play-offs. He told the players, "Men, we talked about geese flying in formation last week. We even tried to run onto the field in formation. Now, men, even though we weren't able to run in the field in formation we played as a team. Our team was in formation men, and when we are a team in formation we can't be beat. Men, I was watching a show this week and a group of gazelle were being chased by hyenas. As long as the gazelle were packed up as a team the hyenas were unsuccessful in catching and killing them. It was as if the hyenas were confused, they didn't know which one to grab there were so many around. But as soon as one of those gazelles broke from the pack the hyenas could focus in on them and they would go after them and eventually catch and kill that gazelle. Men, if we are team nothing can tear us apart. But if we go out their on our own we not only hurt the team but we hurt ourselves. We leave ourselves vulnerable to attack. Men, we are now ranked #4 in this state and we will be attacked. But we've got to stay together, and if we do we cannot fail. Now men, don't take this team lightly. Get out there, play as a team and crush those guys." The players jumped to their feet and rushed out of the locker room. As the players ran out of the room Cleveland looked at Files and said, "That was great!" Out on the fields the captains of each team were gathered with the officials. Coach Holly noticed Jamie's dad in the lower part of the stands at the 50 yard line. Holly walked over to the railing in front of Ed Bridges. Holly motioned for him to come down. "Mr. Bridges. Your boy has had a great year, and I think this football season will continue quite a few more weeks. Only thing that can hurt your son's season is you acting like an idiot. I've not seen you at a game since Southside. Trust me, I've been watching. I'm not sure why you chose tonight to start showing up again and that's your right, but it's not your right to hurt your son. You show the first sign of acting up I'll do everything in my power to keep you from embarrassing that boy." Ed looked at Holly and said, "You don't to worry about that. I'm getting' myself together." Holly replied, "You better. That's a good boy." As Holly walked away Ed called, "Hey, Coach." Holly turned around and Ed called out, "thanks for looking out for my boy." Holly looked at him and replied, "Your boy? I'm looking out for my team," and he walked off.

The players gathered behind the run-through sign. The lights had now been on for about ten minutes. With the game starting late the crowd was growing impatient for the kick-off. Behind the run-through sign Keith gathered the team together and said, "Okay guys. This is our last regular season game of the year. For us seniors, it's the last regular season game that we'll ever play. Let's do what Coach Files says, let's lock hands and run on the field as a team and play as a team." The players all reached out and grasped hands. As Holly walked by he shouted, "What are you doin' back there? Get out there on the field!" So the players began running onto the field. Standing in front of the run-through field was the mascot. He was a student decked out in razorback outfit complete with a large head, tail and red from head to toe. Typically before the players ran through the sign they would do ten jumping jacks, a brief cheer and then run onto the field. With Holly barking out orders the players culled the cheer and just turned and began running onto the field with hands locked together. The mascot waiting in front of the sign intently to hear the cheer was suddenly surprised as the players broke through the sign. As the mass broke through the sign the mascot had no chance to get out of the way or outrun them. The mascot tried to turn and run but fell in front of the mass of humanity. Like dominoes each player began to fall over the mascot. The players had locked hands and were unable to go around the mascot so they began to pile up in a great pile of pink jerseys in front of the run-through sign. The crowd began to laugh as the players got up unsure of what to do at this point. Do you hold hands, do you run, do you just walk, or do you just try to get to the bench and hide hoping that some of the fans had not arrived yet? But with the late start every person seemed to be in their seat waiting for the game. At the bottom of the pile of humanity of pink was the mascot. The usually sleek looking razorback now looked like he had been the loser in a fight with a pit bull. He made his way to the sidelines staggering as though he were leaving a closed down local bar. Holly walked over to Files and said, "Files, why'd you tell the players to dog-pile our mascot? What has he done? Next week are you gonna have them go into the stands and get members of our band? I just don't really understand your motivational techniques, Files." Holly then walked by Dee and said, "Files makes you look good, doesn't he Gordo?"

The game began with Sheridan receiving the kick-off. The first two plays from scrimmage were attempts to run the ball and in both cases the running back was tackled for no gain. Blake Brady blasted through making the first tackle and Keith got the second. On 3rd and 10 the Sheridan quarterback dropped back to pass. The defense began to put pressure on him and Blake Brady was the first to get to him. Blake dropped the quarterback down for an 8 yard loss. Sheridan then punted the ball to Arkansas High and started their first drive from the 50 yard line. Jerome took the hand-off and moved the ball down to the Sheridan 42 yard line. As McAfee came back to the huddle he turned to Jamie and said, "I can run over these guys all night." "Let's do it," Jamie replied. Another play came into the huddle. Jamie changed the play to another running play to McAfee. Jerome picked up another 15 yards down to the 27. Two plays later McAfee had put 6 points on the scoreboard.

By half time the score was 35 to 7, Arkansas High was leading. Cleveland walked into the locker room and said, "Well men, I'm glad you came out to play good football in spite of your coaching staff. That first half was great. Once you finished your pink dog pile of the mascot in front of the run-through sign you really put things together. I don't have much to say other than lets go back out in the second half and pour it on and then we'll let the entire team play before the game is over."

The early part of the second half was similar to the first. Arkansas High took the ball in the opening drive. A few plays later broke a run for a touchdown. Sheridan ran three plays and then punted. By the middle part of the third quarter Arkansas High began substituting freely putting in players from the second and third teams. As the final minutes clicked off the clock several fans began to call to George. George got up from the bench and looked back at the stands. As he did boxes of Twinkies and ho-hos began to rain down on him. George and the other players walked over and picked up the boxes. He spent the final minutes of the game sitting on the bench eating Twinkies and ho-hos. As the last few seconds ticked from the clock box after box of snack cakes were thrown down to the track, each box being scooped up by some of the players.

Everyone on the team had had their fill and George began to gather up the remaining boxes and began to distribute them to cheerleaders and band members and just whoever else might want some.

Cleveland turned and noticed George handing out goodies and turned to Holly and said, "What is that?" Holly looked back at the track and saw George, "You mean the guy in the red and white suit handing out goodies?" He hesitated then continued, "Well actually the suit is," then he screamed, "PINK!" loud enough for Dee to hear. Then Holly continued, "He's about the closest thing to Santa we've got." Cleveland replied, "Tell him to get back over here." Holly replied, "Aw now, Coach, let the boy have some fun. He's not hurting anything. The game's over. We've got the win. He's done a good job for us this year. Let him slide." Cleveland turned his attention back to the field and walked off as the final few seconds ticked off the clock. The coaches stood outside their dressing room in the parking area near the buses. The school secretary, Lisa, had gone and picked up the burgers, fries and cokes for the post-game meal. The coaches were getting the meals ready to hand out to the players. The players slowly began to file out of the locker room. Many of the fans and their kids had also gathered outside of the dressing room for an impromptu kind of pep rally type thing. Keith walked out as one of the first to emerge from the locker room. Some of the kids in the group hollered, "There's Keith!" and ran toward him. Keith stepped out and began to howl. He walked over to the kids and they asked questions like what was it like to hit people so hard and what it felt like to sack a quarterback. Keith began telling the kids about how tough you have to be to play football. He said, "Sometimes they have a big running back who is fast and that big fast guy gets the ball it's like tackling a bear. But if a wolf is tough enough he will throw himself in front of a charging bear and take him down."

The kids attention suddenly turned from Keith to the locker room door. Jerome McAfee began walking out. One of the kids said, "Hey, there's McAfee," and the whole group of kids ran over to Jerome. Keith was left suddenly standing in the dark, alone. "Hey Mr. McAfee, What's it like to score a touchdown?" the kids hollered. "A touchdown?" Jerome replied laughing. "Let's say 'what's it like to score four touchdowns?' You know, when you have one of those break-out games where they can't tackle you." Jerome stooped over as if he was carrying the ball and began to move through the kids like he was running the ball through him. They began to jump in him and try to tackle him. "McAfee can't be brought down," Jerome began announcing. Jerome made his way over to a grassy area and fell on the ground and announced, "Oh the kids are too much for McAfee, they finally bring him down!" The kids laughed and were climbing all over him.

Jamie emerged from the locker room. He was unnoticed as he exited the locker room. The kids were still playing with Jerome and tackling and rolling around in the grass. Jamie loaded his equipment onto the bus. Coach Hollinshead stepped around the corner. "Bridges," Coach Hollinshead said. "I saw your dad at the game tonight." Coach Hollinshead was prying for a little information because although Ed Bridges had come for the start of the game he had left by the time the teams went to half-time. Hollinshead was afraid some of the comments he had made before the game had maybe offended Ed and he had left. Jamie replied, "Yeah, he came to the game. It's the first one in quite a while." Hollinshead then asked, "How come he didn't come and greet you after the game?" He was trying to get information without seeming like he was prying. Jamie replied, "Oh he told me this morning that he would probably stop by the game because he and his girlfriend were going up to Little Rock for the weekend. I figure he left at half time because they wanted to go out to eat and the game got to running long for them so they headed on out." Holly was glad to hear that he had not been the one to offend Bridges and cause him to leave, but was saddened by the fact that there was no more interest in his son's football game than what he had displayed. "Yeah, since Dad found a new girlfriend me and my brother have kind of been on our own. He's got other things to occupy his time lately." Holly then asked, "You think he'll show up for the play-offs?" Jamie hesitated and said, "I'd like to say he would but I really doubt it. He works a lot during the week and the weekend is the only time he has to spend with his lady-friend and so they have been going out a lot. I'm not sure that she's a big football fan anyway." Hollinshead looked at him and kind of sighed for a second and then said, "Well, I'll be there so you better be bringing your A-game!" Jamie kind of laughed and smiled then Hollinshead walked off. A few minutes later the coaches hollered, "Load 'em up!" The players grabbed their sacks of food and loaded onto the buses and headed back for Texarkana.

CHAPTER 12

The Friday night games throughout the state determined the final play off teams and Arkansas High would be playing the Blytheville Chickasaw's. Blytheville is a town in the northeast corner of the state about as far from Texarkana as it is possible to get and stay within the state of Arkansas. Blytheville had finished fourth in their conference and Texarkana had won their conference.

The city of Texarkana was a buzz because three of the four teams in the city had made the playoffs. Arkansas High School had made the playoffs as well as Texas High and Liberty Eylau,. All week long the newspaper talked about the different teams' chances and all three teams were predicted to win the first round of the playoffs. The paper described Blytheville as a team with very fast running backs and a very fast quarterback. James Williams, the writer who the Arkansas High beat, wrote that if Arkansas High could find any way to keep the backs from Blytheville from turning the corner they would win. The Arkansas High coaches also knew this would be a problem. Cleveland sat down with the coaches Sunday afternoon to watch the game films from Blytheville. He stood up after watching the films and said, "Okay guys, we can shut these guys down but we have to make a couple of defensive changes. The way we shut down Blytheville," Cleveland said, "is we get the two ends whenever the ball is snapped to immediately move forward into the back field and turn every play into the heart of our defensive line where we are the strongest. The way Blytheville beat all the teams that they faced is they got to the corner and they turned up field. Speed kills and that's how Blytheville killed all their opponents. If we can cut off the corners Blytheville's speed is neutralized into the middle of the field. Our defensive ends only have to do one thing but they've got to be able to do it well. They've got to be able to get into the back field. They don't have to get to the quarterback or to the running backs but they've just got to get into the back field and turn every play into our linebackers. We do that men and we play another week."

The autumn chill had really set in and the days were growing shorter. The practices weren't as long, partially due to shorter days, but partially also to ensure that the players were well rested and their legs were under them for Friday night. Jamie continued his tradition of staying late after practice with the running backs and the receivers to work on special plays. On Thursday the band, the players and the spirit squad all gathered at Arkansas High Stadium for a pep rally. The band began by playing the National Anthem and the school alma mater. The offensive and defensive starters were all introduced. When the offensive players were called out they lined up on the track in formation of their position on the field. After the entire offense was lined up Jamie was asked to speak to the crowd. He stepped nervously to the microphone and began, "I've really enjoyed my first semester here. I'm amazed at how much better we are as a team compared to how we started the season. We have our coaches to thank for that." A big cheer went up from the fans. When they calmed back down Jamie continued, "This season has been so great and this team has become like a family. I guess I can only say that I only have one regret about this season." The fans sat quietly as Jamie hesitated and then said, "I only regret that there only four more games left for us to win." At that point the fans stood and cheered and the band began to play. The defense was then called out just like the offense. Like the offensive players the defense lined up according to their position and then Keith made his way to the mike. Keith grabbed the mike and howled like a wolf. The crowd howled back then Keith started, "Coach Files told me that a Chickasaw is an Indian, and that's good. 'Cause wolves don't like Indians." The crowd then let out a cheer. Keith then started again, "These coaches and players, they're the baddest around." The crowd let out another cheer. After the crowd quieted Keith said, "We're gonna beat down those Blytheville Chickasaws." Keith then howled and the crowd responded by howling back. The band began to play and after the band played the cheerleaders performed a couple of cheers and soon after that the drill team performed a dance. As the drill team danced Cleveland turned to Holly, "I'm going to introduce the coaches after this. Is there anything you wanna say or do you just want to be introduced?" Holly took a deep breath and said, "Just introduce me." Cleveland looked at Holly and said, "Something wrong? You don't look so good." Holly quickly responded, "Aw I'm fine. I gotta bit of a chest cold kinda rattling in my chest and giving me some problems." After the drill team finished their dance, Cleveland made his way to the mike and introduced his coaching staff. Each of the coaches stood as they were introduced and then sat back down.

Cleveland then turned and faced his team, "I've never been more proud of a football team than I have this one. I challenged this team before the season started to win the state championship. And I'll be honest with you, I thought if we could do better than 500 I'd be happy. Once the season started rolling I could tell we were going to win over half of our games, so I figured if we could make the playoffs that would be great. The season continued and I could see that we were going to make the playoffs. So I adjusted my personal goal for the team. I thought if we could win the conference championship that would be great. Do you know what this group of men did? They did just that. They not only won the conference championship but they won every conference game. I've now made a new personal goal for this team and it's the same as the one that I told them to set for themselves at the beginning of the year, and it's to win the state championship." At that moment the fans stood and cheered as well as did the players and all the coaches except for Holly.

The cheerleaders and the drill team ran onto the track and the band began to play as the cheerleaders and drill team began to dance. Cleveland figured this was a good spot to end his speech and he made his way back to his seat. He again leaned over to Holly, "You sure you're okay?" Holly gruffly responded, "I'm fine. This night air is aggravating my chest cold." As the pep rally came to a close, Doc was called to the microphone and asked to give his rendition of 'Give Me That Old Razorback Spirit'. This is a song sung to the tune of 'That Old Time Religion' and no one could sing it like Doc. The entire crowd came to their feet, locked arms and sang with Doc. He finished the song and the crowd slowly dispersed and the stands emptied. As the people left you could almost hear them humming 'Old Time Religion' as they left.

The following day brought cool temperatures with sun and plenty of wind. Blytheville is an eight hour drive from Texarkana and they arrived about 3:30 in Texarkana and went to the local Sizzler to eat. By 6:30 both teams were on the field and warming up. Coach Files walked over to Cleveland, "Coach, you want me to do the pre-game speech?" Cleveland looked at Files and said, "Coach you did a fine job on the pre-game speeches. Since we're in the playoffs I'd like the chance to do a pre-game talk." "It's because of what happened last week, isn't it?" Files asked. "Look, Files," Cleveland responded, "last week was one catastrophic event after another except for the actual game. I want to just get this game kicked off without a major incident."

The players finished up the pre-game warm up and headed for the locker room. In the locker room there was an air of anxiety that had not been there since the Texas High game. Cleveland walked in and said, "Okay, gather in." The players moved their chairs around and gathered around Cleveland. "Men," he started, "this team's got two things going for 'em. This team we'll face tonight has a tough defense. They're not as good as Texas High but you will earn your yards tonight. The second thing this team's got going for 'em is Blytheville's got speed to burn in the backfield. But men, we've addressed that issue. And if you will just do what you've been taught all week on defense you'll neutralize that speed. Blytheville is very beatable. You're a better team than they are. There is no reason we shouldn't be right here next week." Cleveland turned to the coaching staff and said, "Ya'll have anything?" Holly stood up and began talking, "You seniors need to remember that a loss at this point in the season means your high school career is over." Holly paused and coughed and kind of rubbed his chest and said, "Dern chest cold," then he continued, "I don't want any of you to look back with regret because you gave a half-hearted effort. But I really don't need to tell this team that, do I? I've never seen any of you give anything but your best. That's why you're here. That's why we'll still be playing past Thanksgiving. You men leave nothing in the tank. You put it all out there on the field. So men, keep it up. Let's go get some Chickasaw's!" The players jumped to their feet and headed for the field.

The players congregated behind the run through sign that the cheerleaders were holding. The drill team had formed a sort of runway in front of the football players lining up on each side of the run through sign with the mascot in the middle, but not nearly as close to the run through sign as he had previously lined up at other games. As the coaches made their way toward the sideline beside all the festivities Dr. Compton had walked into the gate. As the coaches passed by Cleveland turned to Holly and said, "Hey, ask Dr. Compton about your cold. He's right there." Dr. Compton perked up and asked, "What can I do for ya?" Holly then replied, "I'm fine. I've just got a little cold that settled in my chest. If it's still hanging on next week I'll come by and get some medicine." "Sounds good," Dr. Compton responded.

Looking over the stadium the visiting team's side fans were low in number due to the length of the trip. They had had a good season but not nearly the season that Arkansas High had had, and there wasn't quite as much excitement surrounding their team. The home side of the stadium was about three-quarters full with people still coming in as the game kicked off. Arkansas High received the ball first and the Chickasaw defense lived up to its name holding Arkansas High to three plays and then a punt. Then the Chickasaws took over and tried twice to run around the end. Each attempt to get to the end was foiled by the defensive ends shooting forward and turning the play into the heart of the defense where the defensive core was waiting.

Much of the first half was a defensive struggle. Both teams would move the ball a little bit but once either team moved anywhere near scoring position the drive would seem to bog down and fizzle. Toward the end of the second quarter Arkansas High's offense began to move the ball. Jamie and the rest of the offense worked the ball down the field into the Chickasaw red zone. On a 2nd and goal play Jerome followed the blocking of Farmer and punched the ball into the end zone making the score 7 to 0 in favor of Arkansas High. That score held up until half time and both teams went into the locker rooms with Arkansas High clinging to a slim 7 to 0 lead.

Cleveland gathered with the defensive players at half time, "Men, I think Blytheville is going to make some adjustments at half time to counter us shooting our ends, so be aware of that. If they do we'll adjust our defense accordingly but I'm not going to stop what we're doing until they begin to have success against us. Men, you have stepped up and I'm proud. Keep playing the way you're playing and we'll live to fight another week. Men, its too early to go home," he said. "We want to play three more weeks." The defense then broke into smaller groups based on position and the different position coaches talked about mistakes made during the first half.

Cleveland then moved to the offense. "Men, we're about to break loose. That touchdown just before half time hurt Blytheville bad. Keep up the pressure and they'll fall apart. Their defensive speed kept them in the game the first half, but our power is going to be the deciding factor in the game. Let's go out there in the second half and just ram it down their throats. If we continue to pound the ball they'll wear down and we'll put them away."

Arkansas High entered the field at the beginning of the second half to the band playing, the fans cheering as loudly as they cheered all game. Since Arkansas High had received the kick to start the first half they kicked off to Blytheville in the second. Much like the first half Blytheville moved the ball for a couple of series and then their drive began to bog down against the Arkansas High defense. Blytheville then lined up to punt the ball to Arkansas High. The punt was a low punt and bounced right into Allen Knight's hands. It was a perfect punt to return a long ways down the field. He caught the ball on the bounce with a full head of steam ran quickly up the right side of the field. Suddenly out of nowhere one of the Blytheville players hammered Knight. He fumbled the ball backward toward his own end zone. There was then a scramble for the ball and Brady came up with the recovery on the Arkansas High 8 yard line. As Knight headed to the sideline Cleveland screamed, "You've got to put the ball away before you get hit! That could've cost us the game." Knight quickly responded, "Coach I never saw him coming. I had running room and then the next thing I knew I was on the ground."

Jamie and the offensive team entered the field with their backs against the goal line. The first play was a running play to McAfee that netted three yards to the 11 yard line. Arkansas High continued to pound running play after running play to Jerome and Farmer. Each play was picking up three to four yards a hit. After what seemed an eternity Arkansas High had moved the ball to the 50 yard line. Knight came to the huddle with another running play called from the sideline. Jamie then glanced toward the bench and said, "Okay guys, lets break 'em right now." The offensive players in the huddle looked with question at Jamie. Then he continued, "I'm going to fake a running play to Jerome. They've seen us run play after play and they think we're going to just keep it on the ground and grind it out. Allen run about ten yards then out and make it just seem like you're getting the cornerback out of the way. As he gets lulled looking for the running play turn it up field. We've lulled them to sleep and now we can go in for the kill." Jamie moved to the line of scrimmage, looked over the defense as he always did, took the snap and moved to give the ball to McAfee and pulled it out. The defensive line swarmed McAfee as they had done on the previous plays. Jamie then put the ball on his hip rolling out. The defense for the moment didn't notice that Jamie still had the ball. Knight ran up field and turned out as the defender got lulled into him running an out pattern he suddenly broke off the pattern and headed toward the goal line. Jamie continued to roll right suddenly pulling the ball up and throwing it down field toward Knight who was breaking away from the defender. Jamie laid up the ball in a perfect pass to Knight who gathered it in and ran untouched into the end zone. Suddenly the 7 to 0 struggle gave way to a little breathing room for Arkansas High with a 14 to 0 score. The offensive players made their way to the side line with Knight grinning from ear to ear. Cleveland caught his eye as he walked passed and said, "Nice catch Knight, but remember you almost cost us earlier, so don't go and get the big head."

The 14 point deficit suddenly took the air out of the Blytheville team. With only a small amount of time left in the third quarter and no points on the board for Blytheville it looked bleak. It had been a defensive struggle for the majority of the game and most of the players realized it was going to be a low scoring game and 14 points could easily win it. The fourth quarter had Arkansas High put another touchdown on the board making the score 21 to 0. The final score ended 21 to 7 when Blytheville scored very late in the game against the second team defense for Arkansas High. With a 21 point lead Cleveland played some of the younger players. As the remaining few minutes ticked away Blytheville was able to take advantage of the younger defense and score their only touchdown.

With the end of the game in sight, the snack cakes began to rain down on the track. As usual several people had boxes especially for George. He walked over and received the boxes and graciously thanked the people for giving them to him. Boxes were thrown all over the track for all the players to gather up. After gathering up the boxes, the players made their way to the middle of the field to shake hands following the game. George began handing Twinkies even to opposing players. He had already handed them out to some of the band members and some of the cheerleaders but still there were so many boxes of Twinkies he had no idea what to do with them. George knew the trip back to Blytheville would be a long one, so he handed them to the other team as well. One by one George gave away the contents of all the boxes that he had. Keith grabbed George and said, "What are you doin? You live for these snacks, like I live for hitting people. Why are you gonna give your stuff away? Are you sick? Were you hit in the head during the game?" George smiled and said, "Naw, Keith. I got so full last week I couldn't eat the rest I had at the game so I gave them away. It was cool. I gave them to the band and the cheerleaders and just whoever wanted them. Those guys, they have a long ride home, so I figured hey, you know, they'll get some McDonald's food before they leave but this will give them a little dessert for the ride. Hey, we've already won, why not be nice to them?" Keith looked at George and said, "George, my friend, I do believe you are crazy." Keith then began to howl and scream. He screamed, "We play another week!" George just smiled looking a Keith celebrate and thought "I'm the crazy one?" He then continued to give away the snack cakes. After all the cakes were gone he followed the rest of the team into the locker room. The players and coaches gathered together in the locker room. Cleveland moved to the front of the team when Files suddenly stepped in. "Hey Denny," Files said, "I want to address the players." Cleveland looked up and said, "Sure, I'll give all the coaches a chance." The players were whooping and hollering. Keith could be heard howling as usual. Cleveland stood and congratulated the team. "Men, I'm so proud of you. Last year we didn't even get to the playoffs. This year you're going to the second round. Men, I'm going to let you in on a little secret. The team we play next week will either be Rogers or Cabot. Men, the secret is they are both very beatable. We have beaten better teams in conference than these two schools. Monday be here and be ready. We'll have a game plan to beat whoever we play, you'll just have to execute. Now, do any of the coaches have anything to say?" Coach Holly stepped forward, "Men, what a special group of guys you are. Do you know what you did tonight?" then he paused, "you didn't do a dang stinking thing that half the teams that played this week did, so don't go get the big head. Don't think you're the greatest in the world. We've won one lousy play-off game. That's not enough for me. I want more." Then suddenly Holly began to cough. He began to hold his chest and then he paused for about 30 seconds. His face almost turned red and some of the players actually became concerned. Then he quit coughing. The he stood as if to catch his breath for a few seconds. Then he muttered, "Dern cold." Then he continued on, "Men, you're better than one round. You can be happy this weekend but be ready to go Monday." Holly looked at Jamie, "Come by my office after you've dressed." Files then stood up and went to get something as Doc and Dee both addressed the players briefly. Files walked back with a large vase. Files walked past Cleveland and Cleveland asked, "What are you doin?" "Oh, David This is cool. I saw the preacher do something similar." Holly looked at Cleveland and said, "I really want to go back to the coaches and find out who we play next week. Call me if my services might be needed here in a few minutes to put out a fire or a snake is in that vase. I can call 911, you know, if this little stunt of Files's goes awry." Files stood up and began, "Men, we've had a great season, haven't we?" The players responded with a loud "Yes sir!" Files continued, "But as Coach Holly said we've got to keep moving forward. Look at this vase, men." It was a big vase sitting in a chair. "This vase is our season so far. Look at the vase, men. Isn't it nice? Isn't the vase pretty?" The players half-heartedly responded, "Yes sir," wondering what in the world Files was trying to tell them. Files then began shouting, "No it isn't! This vase is an ugly piece of junk! Men, if we become complacent with this vase, if we love what we've done so far we won't move on! Men, you know what? I hate this vase, and I hate the second round of the playoffs and I hate conference championships. Men, do you know why I hate these things?" Holly had not made it out of the room coming to Cleveland and said, "Because he's old and senile and was crazy to start with." Files then continued, "I hate these things because they're not what I want. I want a state championship!" The players responded with whoops and cheers. Then Files pulled out a bat and began smashing the vase. The players and coaches sat stunned as he continued to smash the vase into bits. After about a minute or two of smashing there was a trophy at the bottom of the vase. Files reached in and picked up the trophy. "I hate this vase because it's not good enough. I want to trade in this vase for a state title. I want the state title." The players let up a cheer and Keith hollered, "Bust the vase, bust the vase!" The rest of the players began to chant "Bust the vase!" After a few minutes of chanting Cleveland stepped in and said, "Who's got me?" Jamie lifted his hand and he stood and began to pray as the coaches walked away.

After dressing Jamie headed to the coaches office and knocked. A scream, "Come in" was heard. Jamie walked in and the coaches were gathered around the TV checking the scores around the state to see who they would play next week. Jamie spoke up, "Coach Holly, you said you needed to see me?" he said nervously. "Yeah, Jamie," Holly replied, "sit down a minute. Let's find out this score." The station out of Little Rock was rolling through the 5-A scores. The reporter then said, "It was a defensive struggle at Cabot tonight but Cabot was able to defeat the Mounties of Rogers with a final score of 10 to 7." Cleveland said, "Okay coaches. We prepare for Cabot. You know what that's like, 3 yards in a cloud of dust. They won't throw the ball to save their lives." Jamie looked a little puzzled and Holly turned to Jamie and said, "Cabot is the most boring offense you'll ever see in your life. They run the ball 99.9% of the time. Nothing fancy, just push you back slowly down the field. The good thing is that are running into the strength of our defense and our offense is good enough that we can score enough to beat 'em. Come out here Jamie, I want to visit with you." Holly turned to the other coaches and said, "I'll be back. I need to line the boy out." They both walked out onto the practice field. Holly again began coughing for about 30 seconds. He coughed while holding his chest and said, "I'll be glad when this cold gets better." Then he turned and looked at Jamie with a serious look on his face. He said, "My wife asked about you. I told her I'd visit with you and make sure everything is good." Jamie looked puzzled and then said,

"Coach, we just won. It's gotta be good." Holly paused and said, "At home, son. How's everything there? I didn't see you dad tonight." "He was there," Jamie replied. "He's just been dating this lady for a while and she was sitting by him so I guess he decided not to come down after the game." "Do you like her?" Holly asked. "Who?" Jamie responded. Then he said, "Oh, his girlfriend. Yeah, um, when she's around he doesn't drink." Holly interrupted, "I asked you do you like her?" Jamie hesitated and then said rather emphatically, "Well, she isn't Mom. I don't know which is worse his drinking when she's not around or that he could care less about anything concerning us kids when she is around." Holly stood there and looked at Jamie then said, "I'm gonna tell you something. You are to remember it for the rest of your life, alright? You're a good young man. You're as good a young man as I know. I know a lot of people base a lot about the way they feel about themselves on how their dad treats 'em. But I tell you right now, you're an outstanding young man. I'd call you mine any day. So whatever that's worth you take it and remember it. Oh, yeah. One other thing, the coaches are going to be looking at the Cabot films this Sunday. We'll grade 'em out and we'll get an idea about what kind of defense we're gonna face. Monday why don't you and me get together up here and we'll go over those same films I'll show you what we're seeing and you can kind of see what you'll be facing." Jamie quickly responded, "I'd like that Coach." Then Coach Holly smiled and said, "Okay, get outta here Goober." Jamie smiled, walked to his truck and headed home.

CHAPTER 13

Jamie drove to school Monday, he got out of his car and headed toward the locker room wondering exactly what the players would be doing, whether they'd be watching game films or maybe going through a few plays in shorts outside. He entered the locker room and several players were sitting around in school clothes. Jamie looked at George and said, "Are we watching films this morning?" George replied, "I don't know. Cleveland said to stay in street clothes and just wait here for the coaches." As the players filed in one by one more and more questions circulated about this morning's practice. Many of the players were still excited about the win on Friday night and the chance they would get to play in the second round this week against Cabot. Once all of the players were in the locker room Cleveland, the other coaches and Mr. Rice as well as Mr. Pope, the school's principals entered the room. Everything was pretty normal but the principals. They had never come down to a morning practice. Every once in a while they would show up in the afternoons just to say hello and watch a few minutes of practice but never had they been in here in the morning. Cleveland looked around and said, "Men, something terrible has happened." He hesitated to compose himself, "I don't know any other way except to just come right out and tell ya." There was a long hesitation, "At 5:00 this morning Coach Holly got up and walked into his den and he collapsed and died of a heart attack. His wife called me this morning and said that he got up with his chest hurting and he was coughing. She fell back asleep and then got up to check on him and he had collapsed and died." There was not a sound in the entire room. Jamie then calmly got up and walked toward the door. Cleveland looked at Jamie and said, "Bridges, you okay?" Jamie didn't even acknowledge he had heard him. He opened the door and walked out. Cleveland motioned for Dee to follow him. The door closed behind Dee and Cleveland turned back to the rest of the team and said, "Men, the coaches and principals are here to talk with ya." Dee suddenly looked back in the room and said, "Coach, he's gone." Cleveland replied, "Who?" "Jamie," Dee said quickly. He just took off running. Cleveland quickly stepped out of the locker room to see Jamie running to his car, get in and drive away. Cleveland walked back into the silent locker room. Mr. Rice began to make his way to visit with some of the players. He told them what a loss it was and told the players that all of the coaches and principals would be available to talk this week. Mr. Pope turned to Cleveland. "What do we need to do about Bridges?" he asked. "I can have the truancy officer look him up." "No," Cleveland quickly responded, "the kid's done nothing wrong. We'll handle this within the team." Doc walked over to Cleveland, "If you want I'll go find him." Cleveland then looked at Doc and asked, "You know where he is?" Doc said, "I got a sneakin' suspicion. Not many places for him to go." Cleveland thought a minute and said, "Yeah, go get him before he gets into trouble."

The players sat quietly and visited among themselves with the coaches and principals. Keith walked over to Cleveland and said, "Coach, this is probably the wrong time to ask, but what about the game this week?" Cleveland then stood and addressed the team, "Keith has asked a good question. He asked about the game this week. I am going to check with the State's Activities Association and find out if we can postpone the game. I don't think we could make any schedule changes since it is playoff game, but I still want to check. So in all likelihood the schedule will not change. This leaves us with a decision. I want you to vote as a team whether or not we play this week. I'm standing here looking at a group of renegades that have developed into a team, but more importantly a group of fine young men. Men, if you think it will be too difficult to play this week I'll understand and we can call them and forfeit. On the other side if you feel like Holly would want you to play that will be fine too. One request I have is that if you decide to play you've got to be committed to playing this entire week. We will still practice and we will still prepare." McAfee then spoke up, "What about the funeral?" Cleveland replied, "They're making those plans right now. We will go as a team to the funeral. Okay, let's go ahead and let's take care of this vote. I want all heads down and eyes closed. Coaching staff and myself will also close our eyes. Mr. Rice you count the votes. Do not tell anyone how the kids voted. Mr. Rice, I mean, I do not want anyone to know how any person in here voted, not even myself. If later on I ask you, you don't tell me. So if you would, go ahead." Mr. Rice then stepped forward, "Alright men, all heads down, all eyes closed. If you do not feel like it would be right to play this week raise your hand." After a pause he said, "Okay, if you feel like Holly would want the game to be played and you want to play in it, raise your hand." There was another long pause. Then Mr. Rice said, "Okay, hands down. You can raise your heads and open your eyes." Cleveland looked over and said, "Okay, what's the verdict?" Rice replied, "Holly would want us to play so we'll play." Cleveland said, "Okay men, we'll spend the remainder of this class talking about this issue and you'll have opportunities all week to discuss Holly's death with coaches, principals or other faculty. This afternoon we'll be on the field preparing for Cabot." Knight then spoke up, "Coach, what about Bridges?" Cleveland hesitated and then bit his lip. The reality of the situation almost seemed to hit him all at once with that question. He drew a couple of deep breaths and tried to answer, then turned and walked off. Files quickly spoke up, "Doc will take care of Bridges. He'll be ready to roll this afternoon."

Doc drove his car out toward the spillway. During the summer months people would be lined up along the spillway but today there was only a single figure carrying a bow. Jamie made his way up and down the spillway and occasionally he'd let an arrow fly. With the sound of the water rushing through the spillway, and the constant crashing of the water onto the rocks, Jamie had not noticed the car driving up. As Doc climbed out of the car Jamie shot a fish. The fish was large and putting up quite a fight. Jamie was moving up and down the rocks trying to get the fish. By the time Jamie landed the fish Doc was behind him. Doc spoke up and said, "Son of a gun, that one's mine or I'll turn you in for skipping class." Jamie jerked, startled by the voice thinking he was alone. He looked back down at the fish, "Yeah, you can have it. I just wanted to shoot something. I don't want to keep it." The wind was damp and cold coming off the spillway. Doc spoke up and said, "This ain't exactly good fishin' weather." Jamie began getting the arrow out of the fish. Once the arrow was out he looked at Doc and said, "You want me to keep it in my cooler in the car and I'll bring it to your house later. I figure you don't have anything to put it in." Doc replied, "Yeah, that'll be fine. Bring it to the school. I'll get a cooler out of the training room." There was a long pause. Jamie just stared down the spillway. After about four or five minutes he suddenly blurted out,

"He knew he didn't have a cold. He knew he was having heart problems. Dang it, he knew it! That's why he was talking to me after the game Friday night. He was making sure I was going to be okay." Jamie paused and then screamed at the top of his lungs, "He knew it!" There was a long silence and then Doc spoke up and said, "So he did. Look Son, Holly didn't let many people get close to him. For some reason he let you. He liked you. Something about you, he felt like you were his. Every game during the week we'd talk about how a team could beat us but Holly would always come back with 'Yeah, but we've got Bridges. Bridges will get us what we need to win.' We'll all miss him. I know you'll miss him as much as anyone. Even though he is gone he would want you to go on. That's probably why he talked with you Friday night." Jamie then quickly replied, "They're all gone! They're all gone! All of them, they're all gone! Not a single one is left. Mom is gone, Dad might as well be gone and now Holly's gone." Although he wasn't sobbing a tear rolled down his face and Doc then said, "You liked him, I know he liked you. Yeah, I bet you'd want to make him happy, right?" "Yeah," Jamie slowly responded as if wondering where the conversation was going. Doc then continued, "I know the thing that makes us coaches feel better than winning a conference championship is seeing a kid that we helped do well. I can guarantee you that pay is not why we coach. Winning is fun, but it's really not why we coach. We wouldn't put up with what we have to if winning were the only thing we got out of it. We're trying to invest some of ourselves into someone else. For some reason Holly chose his investments carefully. He didn't invest in many, but I think he invested wisely. Now, how can you you make his investment pay off?" Jamie stood still looking down the spillway. Then he responded, "I don't know." Doc said, "Well, I can't speak for Holly. I feel good when I see a son of a gun go and make something of himself. I'm not talking about becoming a pro athlete or president or anything like that. I mean a person who is respected, cares for his family and takes care of others. Heck, many of those guys I've seen that made it to the pros are egotistical jerks. If you give up on life because of his death I can guarantee you that he wouldn't be happy." Jamie then turned and said, "So what do I do?" Doc said, "You remember him but you move on. Then when you see him in Heaven you tell him he was a big part of the reason you became what you became." There was a long silence then Jamie responded, "Alright." Then Doc said, "Look son of a gun, I'm cold." Jamie replied, "I'm gonna shoot one more fish and then I'll get back to school." Doc then said, "Alright, I'm trusting you." Doc then climbed into his car and rode off. Jamie began to look for another fish.

Practice resumed that afternoon. Jamie had returned to the school after lunch. Practice was quiet and somber but the players knew they had to endure practice if they had any hopes of winning. The players gathered together after practice and had a team prayer. Cleveland stood in the middle of the players and began speaking, "Men, they've scheduled Holly's funeral for tomorrow at 1:00. School will be let out to allow any of the students who want to attend the funeral to go. We'll meet here and we'll gather as a team. I want you all to look nice. As far as the game Friday they won't reschedule. I talked with the rules committee and they said the times cannot change. I'm not going to mandate that we have practice tomorrow. I am going to be here, so will the coaches, but practice tomorrow will be voluntary. If you do not feel you can practice after the funeral it will not be held against you." Following practice Jamie went by the coaches office and he knocked. A voice from inside called, "Come in." Jamie entered the office and said, "Coach Cleveland, Holly said he would have some tapes up here for the Cabot game for me to look at so I could look at the defense." Cleveland got up and said, "Let's see. Let's see if he left anything on his desk." Cleveland walked over to the other office area and began to fumble around on the desks. He grabbed two VCR tapes and said, "Yep, here they are." He walked back over to Jamie and said, "Have a seat." Cleveland and Jamie both sat down. Cleveland started, "So, you doin' okay?" Jamie fidgeted a little bit, "Yeah, I'm gonna be okay." There was a silence that was just about to get uncomfortable when Cleveland finally broke it by saying, "Hard to understand when God takes good people. Holly was one of the best. I've coached with him now for almost ten years. He always kept a good perspective on things. He wanted to win, don't get me wrong, but he knew there was more to life than football. I really feel for his wife, 'cause he probably would have retired in a few more years and I know they had planned to do a lot of traveling." Jamie just kind of nodded. Cleveland then said, "So Holly wanted you to look at the game films, huh?" "Yes sir," Jamie replied, "he thought I'd be more comfortable if I knew what the defense looked like." "You want to do that?" Cleveland asked. "I do," Jamie replied. "Maybe I'll pick up some weaknesses or tendencies that might help us Friday night, I don't know." Cleveland smiled and said, "Yeah, life goes on even after death. Well, enjoy the tapes. If you need me for anything let me know. You've got my home number so give me a call if you have any questions or you just want to talk." "Thanks, Coach," Jamie said, then he made his way out of the coaches office.

The funeral was packed. It seemed as though the entire school had turned out. The football team sat together with all the players wearing white button downs and a tie. The preacher talked a while followed by one of Coach Holly's friends from the military. The funeral then proceeded to the cemetery for a brief grave side service. Coach Holly's wife walked over to the football team following the service and said, "You boys will never know how much you meant to Bill. He considered you his own kids. You brought joy to his life." Tears began to stream down her face. "He would want you go out this week and not worry about him and play the best you possibly can Friday night." She then began to cry and motioned the players could go on and get back to the bus. Jamie was one of the last to leave the side of the casket. He made his way to the bus. Coach Holly's wife walked over and hugged him and whispered, "You were his favorite. He told me he considered you his son. I thank you for being so good to him." "Ma'am," Jamie replied, "I wish I could have been half as good to him as he was to me. You don't know how much I miss him."

CHAPTER 14

Friday night finally arrived after what seemed to be the longest week of the season, including two-a-days. The players had received black stickers with a white H on them to wear on their helmets in honor of Coach Holly. The mood and intensity of practice had picked up each day after the funeral. Coach Holly's death had brought a lot of publicity to the team and it seemed as though the entire city had come out to watch the game. The home side bleachers were filled with Arkansas High fans. The visitor's side was over half full with a mixture of Cabot and Arkansas High fans who could not find seating on the home side. Arkansas High fans had staged a mini-pep rally and tailgate party before the start of the game. The band and spirit squads were out in full force.

Files had approached Cleveland earlier in the week about the pre-game speech. Cleveland said, "Files I appreciate you wanting to do this, but this talk's gotta be mine." The players were all gathered in the dressing room as Cleveland and the rest of the coaching staff entered. "Men," Cleveland began, "I told you last week was the most important game of your lives, and it was. But guess what men? This week is the most important game in your lives. And next week will be the most important game of your lives. The first thing you need to remember out there is not to leave anything on the field. Every bit of energy you have, every bit of guts, every bit of drive needs to be put out there on the field. If we lose, it's over. Don't go home tonight saying, "if I'd tried a little harder." If we lose tonight I want you going home tonight saying 'we gave it all we could and we got beat by a better team'. But men, I'll tell you this. If we put everything out there on the field that we've got in us I can guarantee you we'll win. Men, those guys aren't fancy. They're in your face smash mouth football. If they get a 14 point lead they're hard to beat because the offense they run just burns the clock. You've got to come out of the blocks good. We can't wait until the second half to decide to play football. Men, I want you know no matter what happens tonight I cannot be more proud of a team. Early in the season I'd hoped to win half of our games and now we're in the second round of the playoffs against a team I really think we can beat. I know many of you have said that you want to play the game for Coach Holly, and that's great. But I also want you to play it for yourselves. Men, Holly loved football, but what he loved more was seeing kids succeed. You gave Holly something special. He was able to see a team who was an underdog win all year long. He saw kids that were underdogs step up. He saw George go from not playing at all to being the heart of this offensive line. He saw Keith go from an injury prone kid to one of the most dominant defensive players in our conference. He saw Bridges, who had not played for us before, take this team to the second round of the playoffs." Cleveland paused as tears began to well up in his eyes. He tried to speak again but couldn't. He walked out of the locker room and Doc stepped in the front and said, "Alright men, you have your marching orders now get out there and kick those sons of a gun around like rag dolls."

The game began with Cabot receiving the opening kickoff. As expected they pounded the running game right at Arkansas High. The defense gave up two first downs and then held. After the punt Arkansas High's offense stepped on the field. Jamie stepped into the middle of the huddle and said, "Alright, we're gonna bust them hard early. Coach called a handoff to McAfee. Let's just fake it. Knight, you go to block your man and then roll off him and head toward the end zone. I'll find you." Jamie faked the handoff to McAfee. The Cabot defense swarmed him. Jamie then dropped back keeping the ball on his hip. Knight then sold the block to the cornerback and was able to scrape off of him and break away from him. Jamie threw a pass hitting him in mid-stride. With both defenders almost ten yards behind him Knight made the catch and ran the rest of the length of the field for a touchdown. The offense ran off the field and Cleveland grabbed Jamie and said, "What was that, I called a run?" Jamie quickly responded, "Coach I watched that corner get burned in every game and I knew Knight could beat him." Cleveland then smiled and said, "Keep up the good work, Son."

Both teams were unable to drive the ball at times but neither was able to score through the rest of the first quarter and most of the second. Toward the end of the quarter Arkansas High drove the ball down to the Cabot 15 yard line. Jamie took the snap and pitched the ball to McAfee and he ran around the left end, bounced off the cornerback and into the end zone. Arkansas High added the extra point to make it a 14 to 0 game. Arkansas High then kicked to Cabot and the remaining time before half time ticked off the clock. Cleveland entered the locker room at half time and shouted, "Men we're on our way! This team we're playing scores very slowly. If you can come out and get a quick score we'll have the game under control. The remainder of the half time was spent making minor adjustments to some of the things that Cabot had shown them in the first half. Cleveland stood up just before the players went back on the field and said, "Men, leave nothing in the tank. Put everything out there on the field. If you'll do that we'll be here again next week one week closer to a state title."

Arkansas High received the kick off to start the second half. Jamie began to pick on the cornerback that he had burned on the first play of the game. Since that play the cornerback was playing way off the receiver to ensure he didn't get burned again. Jamie began throwing short pass after short pass to that side of the field. Each pass was netting between 10 and 15 yards. Steadily Arkansas High was marching down the field. Once inside Cabot's 30 yard line runs to McAfee and Farmer were mixed in until finally Farmer punched the ball in the end zone on a 2 yard dive play. A 21 point deficit would be a difficult task for almost any team to overcome, but a running team like Cabot could be near impossible.

The game ended with the score 21 to 0. The track again was littered this time with literally hundreds of boxes of snack cakes. Some of the players grabbed their boxes. George went out and got the ones from the fans who had handed them specifically to him and graciously again thanked them. He then began carefully stacking other boxes behind the bench. The fans ran onto the field along with the cheerleaders and drill team. Coach Cleveland gathered the team around. George was one of the last ones to make it to the meeting in center field after he had stacked his boxes. Cleveland shouted, "Men I cannot describe this. You have surpassed every expectation I had for you. I don't know what to say. Holly would be proud of you, men. I'm proud of you men. The whole coaching staff is proud of you. I know Holly's looking down from Heaven at this game grinning from ear to ear. So men, celebrate this weekend and

Monday let's get ready for next week. Then State men. We're one game away from playing to see who's the best in the state." The team then gathered in tighter and said a prayer, then began to move off the field. George ran over to Coach Desrochers, "Coach, Coach. Can I get your help?" "Sure George, what is it?" Dee replied. "Well Coach, all of these people brought snack cakes. The players got what they wanted and I gave some away to the cheerleaders and the players from Cabot, but there are still 60 or 70 boxes. I don't know what to do with them all." Dee stood and thought a moment and said, "Let me think. Hey," after a long pause, "how about you and I take a trip to the homeless shelter. The boxes aren't open, right?" George replied, "No Coach. They aren't open. They may be dented a little bit from people throwing them on the track but they're not open." Dee then screamed, "Sophomore maggots get over here!" Sophomore players who had not played the game night ran over to Coach Desrochers. "Men," Dee said, "I want all of these boxes in the back of my truck." One of the sophomores laughed, "You sure are hungry, huh?" Dee replied, "Just shut up and do it maggot." Dee then turned to George, "You want to go with me?" "Sure," George replied. Dee said, "Okay, get your shower. I'm gonna go check some scores in the coaches' office while you're showering. When you get finished come to the coaches' office and then we'll go."

The coaches were gathered around the TV in the coaches' office watching the news again out of Little Rock to find out who they play next week. J. A. Fair was a high school in Little Rock. It would be either them or Bentonville, a school out of the northwest corner of the state that would be the next team that Arkansas High would face. The announcer began going through the 5A scores. He mentioned that Texarkana has beaten Cabot. Just then there was a knock heard on the door. All the coaches screamed, "Come in!" in unison. George walked in. Dee looked around and said, "Yeah, come in George. Have a seat for a minute. They're about to get to the Bentonville game. While we're waiting on the score, have you called your mom and told her you're going with me?" "Yes sir," George replied. The announcer then came on with the J.A. Fair/Bentonville game. He said, "Tonight in Bentonville, Arkansas the running attack of J.A Fair finally was slowed down by the

Bentonville defense. Bentonville wins 35 to 31." "Alright fellas," Cleveland said, "it's Bentonville." Dee spoke up and said, "Hey Coach, George here and I are going to take these Twinkies to the homeless shelter." "Sounds good," said Cleveland. Then Cleveland turned to George and said, "George, you're getting to be quite a celebrity, aren't you?" George shyly looked up at Cleveland and said, "Well I, I guess so," then turned and walked out.

George and Dee arrived at the homeless shelter. They walked into a large room and several people were gathered around the TV. Dee and George walked to the desk and asked the man who was sitting there if they could leave some food. After a small conversation Dee and George left and then re-entered with the boxes of snack cakes. People around the TV began to applaud these two big guys bringing gifts of food. One of the kids in the group looked to be about a few years younger than George said, "Hey, bring me some of that." George then looked at the receptionist, "Can I give some out?" "Sure you can," the receptionist responded. George then grabbed a couple of boxes and began handing out the snack cakes. After giving the snacks all around the room to anyone who wanted them, the receptionist said, "There's another room in the back. Let me go back there and see if anybody wants some." The receptionist returned a few minutes later and motioned for George to come back to that area. As George walked in he noticed the area had more women and kids. The kids went wild as George handed out the food. George had never felt so good in his life. His team had just won in the second round of the playoffs, but that paled in comparison to seeing all of these kids light up when he handed them a bed-time snack. One of the kids then spoke up and asked George if he was Santa Claus. George replied, "Oh, no. I'm just a football player." The room suddenly became more excited. One of the boys spoke up and said, "Did you play tonight?" "I sure did," George replied. "Did you win?" another one asked. "We did," George replied. The kids then all said, "Tell us about the game, tell us about the game!" George then sat down on the couch and all of the kids gathered around him. He began telling them about the game emphasizing how he and the offensive line had driven Cabot off the ball and opened holes all night. As he finished telling the story Dee poked his head in the room and motioned for George to come on.

George then quickly said, "We won the game and we play again next week." The kids began to yell, "Come back next week," to which George replied, "I will. I'll be back next week. I'll see ya next Friday night." George walked out with Dee and climbed into the truck with him. Dee looked over and said, "You have a good time?" "Man, that was so cool. That was the best. I mean winning is fun, but man, that was the best!" "You really going back next week?" Dee asked. "Man, I got to. I gave them my word," George said. "Those kids are expecting me. Will you go with me?" Dee then paused a moment and said, "Next week if you need a ride I'll provide it, but the rest of it's on your own." "Alright," George replied.

CHAPTER 15

The following Monday practice still had a feeling of a void with Holly not being on the field. The void was slightly numb with the players knowing they were one game away from the state championship game. This would be a strange practice week because Thanksgiving day was on Thursday. There would no school on either Thursday or Friday. Liberty Eylau had been beaten the previous week and were out of the playoffs, but Texas High was still alive. Texas High would have to win three more games for a state title compared to the two Arkansas High would have to win. Coach James from Texas High and Cleveland got together on the phone and decided to have a combined pep rally on Thursday night. It was decided the pep rally would be held at 7:30 at Arkansas High stadium. The community would be invited and it would be an event trying to drum up support for both teams.

As Monday's practice came to a close Cleveland stood in front of the players. The day was cool and cloudy and there was a light mist falling, as you get often times in late fall. The trees had all turned from a reddish orange to more of a brown and were beginning to lose their leaves. "Men," Cleveland said, "today was the best practice we've had all year. This week will be practice as usual today, tomorrow and Wednesday. But since Thursday is Thanksgiving we'll practice at 8:00 in the morning. We'll go for about an hour, just kind of go through a pre-game and touch up a few things we need to work on, then you'll have plenty of time at home to have Thanksgiving dinner with your families. That night we'll have a pep rally at 7:30. It will be a combined pep rally with Texas High with their team, their spirit groups and their fans will all come over as well as ours, so it will be a big community event. I know I've told you this several times year, but again, this Friday night will be the biggest game of your lives. Two weeks ago I told you it was the biggest game of your lives and you won that one. Each week they get bigger. No let ups this week, men. We need to stay focused and make sure we do everything possible this week to put ourselves in the best position to win this game. Leave no doubt that you did everything you could to win. Now who's got me?" George raised his hand and stood up and began to pray. The practice ended with whoops and celebration as the players ran off the field and into the dressing room.

   Each successive practice went better than the one before. Tuesday's practice the kids seemed even more focused and ready for the game as well as they did Wednesday. Thursday night brought about the city wide pep rally. The teams and spirit groups from both schools were there along with almost 500 community supporters. The parents of not only the players but the spirit groups, and then some just who had stayed in town for the Thanksgiving Holiday and were interested to see what was going on. It was interesting that the two teams who had hated each other so fiercely during the first game of the season would come together tonight and celebrate the season that each one of them had had and to cheer each one on hopefully to victories Friday night. As the pep rally began George walked up and Dee stopped him and said, "Where have you been? You're late." "Alright, Coach" George responded, "I went to the shelter to help serve Thanksgiving dinner. Man, Coach. That place is so great. I love those kids. I mean those kids have it bad but still they're good kids." "That's great George," Dee responded. Get down there with your teammates. Don't be late again or you'll run for it." "Okay Coach," George replied. The bands each played the alma matters followed by the teams' fight songs. The cheerleaders performed a couple of cheers of their own and then after each cheerleading group had performed their own cheers both groups came together and performed a few cheers together. The drill teams from each school performed separate routines. The week had not afforded enough time for the drill teams to get together and have a routine together. The bands both played and then both coaches came to the microphone. First to the mic was Coach James from Texas High. As Coach James stepped to the mic he talked about how his team was right where he expected them to be all year long. He said that even during summer practice he knew that his team was going to be one that would step up. He continued saying that even though there were ups and downs they would fight through and be a team that would be a contender for a state championship. He told the crowd gathered there that this Thanksgiving was great and he was very thankful for everything that he had. He ended by saying that he knew he would be even more thankful come Friday night when he knew that he was in the third round of the playoffs and had only two games left before they would be the state champions of 4A in Texas. The fans cheered and Texas High's band played as Coach James made his way back to his chair. Cleveland slowly got up and made his way to the microphone. As Cleveland got to the microphone the crowd quieted down. As he began he started by saying this season had been nothing like what he expected. He said when he looked at his team this summer he saw a rag-tag group of kids. He never expected the team to come together as they had be one of the best in the state of Arkansas. He said how he could not be more proud of a group of men who couldn't even make the playoffs last year but now are in the thick of the race for a state championship. He said there were many obstacles that Arkansas High had faced this year but none as the big as the loss of Coach Holly last week to a heart attack. At this point he stopped and hesitated, almost biting his lip. You could almost hear a pin drop as he regained his composure to start again. He then started again and said that he could not be more proud of the team. He then turned to the players and looked at them with a serious look on his face and said, "This team knows what these next two games mean not only to them, but to the community and the school as a whole." He said, "I can guarantee you one thing, these men will fight with everything that they have. Win or lose they'll walk off the field knowing they did everything they could to be state champions. And I believe they will be state champions." He walked away from the mic as the Arkansas High band began to play and the cheerleaders performed another routine.

Friday afternoon finally came. As the players were gathered in the locker room getting dressed, getting the equipment together and having the final team chats the fans were gathering outside of the stadium. There was a great amount of electricity in the air. The booster club had scheduled a tailgate party before the game. Hamburgers and brauts were being cooked on a giant grill. Several members of the band had gathered to play while the cheerleaders and drill team also performed. The cheerleaders led the band in a cheer of calling the hogs. The band played a while and then after several of the members of the state play off team of 1974 got up and recalled memories from the year they had won the state championship. Tonight the evening was clear. The temperatures would drop into the mid to high 40s by the end of the game. During the tailgate party, while Arkansas High was getting dressed, Bentonville was also unloading and getting dressed. Bentonville was about a five hour drive from Texarkana. The fans had chartered a couple of busses and during the tailgate party those busses began to pull into the parking lot. As the Arkansas High players made their way toward the stadium the fans began to line up along the gate where the players would enter the field. The fans made a large pathway for the players to run through and cheered as each player made their way onto the field. The tailgaters let out many cheers, the cheerleaders jumped and did back handsprings while the band played. The players made their way onto the field to begin their warm-up activities and noticed a huge picture of the state of Arkansas with the letters AHS across it had been painted in the middle of the field. Win or lose this would be the last game played that year at Arkansas High Stadium. If they won, next week the state championship game would be played in Little Rock. If they lost the season would end. Two of the booster club members had gotten together and since it was going to be the last game that year, painted the outline of the state on the field with the letters across it. Jamie walked onto the field along with Farmer right behind him. He looked over his shoulder at Farmer and almost nervously said, "Man, they are serious about this." Farmer quickly responded as he was skipping onto the field, "Heck, yeah! 'Cause we're going to be in the state championship game next week. This is dead dog serious!" McAfee came running past the two jumping and shouting, "We're gonna have some fun tonight, fellas! I feel it baby!" Cleveland and the rest of the coaching staff slowly made their way onto the field as well. Cleveland looked over at the other coaches and said, "The hardest part of this game is going to be keeping the players calm enough to play this game. This is one of those times when we really need Holly. Holly would walk into a locker room, tell some crazy story or dumb joke and get the kids focus back. He then would chew them out about acting stupid." "Yeah," Dee responded. "Remember last year before the Texas High game the kids were so nervous we couldn't get a play off in warm-ups. You hollered across the room and told Holly to tell the kids a joke?" "Yeah," Cleveland interrupted, "and then he said he didn't know any clean ones." Then Cleveland continued, "That was great 'cause the kids laughed and relaxed just enough to be able to get out there and play. We got beat but we played okay." Files then spoke up, "Hey, I know," Cleveland quickly cut Files off with a sharp, "NO! Files, I don't even want to hear it." The other coaches laughed and walked off to begin work with the players.

The players finished their warm-up routine and then made their way into the locker room. The bands and fans were revved up and had made their way to the seats. Only during the Texas High game had there been so much energy before a game this season. Inside the locker room was a combination of great excitement and anticipation but also a degree of fear. Each player knew that this game could be a big step to the state championship game in Little Rock or the end of the season, the season that no player wanted to see end. Each week the practices had become more fun. Each week just knowing a game was awaiting them made school actually fun. The entire campus had become mesmerized by football. The newspaper daily had articles on either different players or about the opposing team. The faculty members who normally didn't like football were actually following the team each week. This next week could be either another page in this dreamy season or be the end of it all.

The locker room was quiet. The players were seated as Cleveland walked into the room with the other coaches. One of the camera men from a local TV station had asked to film some of the pre-game activities including the pre-game speech. As the coaches came in he entered as well with his camera and made his way to the back of the room. Normally this would have created much excitement and would have been quite a distraction, but the players were so focused on Cleveland and the game they barely noticed the cameraman come by. Cleveland paced nervously around the old room. The smell as usual was a musty, damp smell. The locker room was very old and had old wood floors. The floors had that dry, dusty and musty smell from the sweat of every player that had come through Arkansas High. Cleveland continued to pace and almost seemed that his pacing made the excitement of the players go up a level. Outside the locker room the players could hear the muffled sound of the band playing. Every once in a while they would hear the PA announcer speak to the fans overhead. Cleveland suddenly stopped his pacing and turned toward the team. He looked at them for a moment and then began, "Men, when I was a boy I would go to the circus with my dad. We loved it when the circus came to town. One of the things I liked best was going the day before the circus started. Dad would take me down there and people could come out and watch the elephants put up the big tent. Men, I don't know if you've ever been around an elephant, but it is a giant, giant creature. And these big elephants would grab these big poles and they would move the poles and anything else that needed to be moved to set up the tent. The men who trained the elephant would just walk beside them and would cue them as to what to do. We watched as these elephants moved each pole into place. And these weren't small poles. These were big telephone pole type things. These elephants would pick them up and throw them around like they were toothpicks. Then they would move the poles into place so they could stand them up and connect the tent to it. They would drive the stakes into the ground around the tent and they would have it all put up. Then something interesting would happen. You know what that was? The guy who was training the elephant would take a 4 foot stake and drive it into the ground. Then he would take the rope that was attached to the elephant and wrap it around the stake and tie it. Now think about it, men. These elephants just moments ago were taking objects that weighed hundreds and hundreds of pounds and move them into place so they could put up this tent. Then this guy would drive a small 4 foot stake in the ground and the elephant couldn't get away. Men, do you know why they couldn't get away?" Cleveland gave a long dramatic pause to add to the story not expecting an answer when Keith suddenly shouted, "Hey Coach. I once peed on one of them shocker fences and it knocked fire from me. I thought I was gonna die. I bet somebody took one of them shocker sticks they got and poked them two or three times. Two or three times of getting shocked I think that'd stop an elephant from moving a stake." All the other coaches began to bite their lips to keep from laughing. Dee had to walk out of the locker room. The cameraman was still perched in the back of the room and began to shake trying to control his laughter. Cleveland looked at Keith and said, "Not exactly Keith." Then there was another lengthy pause as Cleveland re-gathered his thoughts. In the back of his mind he was glad Holly wasn't in on this speech because he knew there would've been a comment from Holly that would have completely destroyed the rest of the speech. Cleveland then said, "Men the reason the elephant can't move the stake or get loose is that he doesn't think he can." Then he paused. After a dramatic pause he continued, "Men, when that elephant was a baby they would drive the stake into the ground and tie him to it and he really couldn't pull loose when he was younger because he was much smaller. As the years went by they continued to tie him to the same stake and the elephant quit trying to pull because when he was younger he had tried and tried and realized he couldn't do it. But as he got older, bigger and stronger he never tried again, not realizing that he had become strong enough and big enough to yank that stake from the ground like it was a toothpick. Men, we haven't won a state championship at this school in a very long time. There are people saying that we can't do it just because it has been so long. But men, we are one game away from that game. Just like that elephant could pull the stake from the ground if he just thought he could, we can be state champions, if you think you can. It's all in the mind, men. You're as good, if not better, than any of the teams we are going to face this week and next week. And if you decide you can do it, we will be state champions." He paused briefly and then screamed, "Now get out there and play like state champions." The players jumped to their feet and quickly headed out the door toward the field.

As the teams entered the field both crowds cheered loudly. The home stands were full of red and white. The visitor's side of the stadium was three-fourths full with Bentonville fans, but a few of the Arkansas High fans had spilled over onto that side because the home side was full. The weather was perfect for fans to bundle up in a blanket with some hot chocolate and watch the football game.

Everything seems more intense in the playoffs. The band seems to play louder. The stadium lights seem to be brighter. The crowd seems to react more often and louder to each play. Even the hamburgers being cooked behind the concession stand smelled better. Keeping with the theme of being more intense, the cheerleaders had created a large run through sign with a razorback running across the state of Arkansas and the sign read, "The

conference championship was great but we're running for state."
Coach Files lined up behind the sign with the players. Cleveland
wanted to let Files still be involved in the pre-game to keep from
hurting his feelings and he felt the best way to keep a catastrophe
from occurring was to have a coach run through the sign with them.

The bands finished playing their respective alma mattas and
attention turned to the two teams waiting behind the run through
signs. Bentonville entered the field followed by Arkansas High.
Cleveland thought to himself how crazy it was to be concerned about
how the kids would run onto the field. But after having several
games begin by the players embarrassing themselves and the school
by not being able to run onto the field, that there was definite need
for concern with this group of guys. It wasn't like the fields were
uneven or sloppy wet either. The fields were perfectly dry and
smooth. It was amazing that a group of gifted athletes couldn't run
on a well manicured carpet of grass. There was the sound of
popping and tearing when the players tore through the sign and make
their way onto the field to great cheers from both sides of the
stadium. The Arkansas High team made it onto the field without
incident. Cleveland breathed a sigh of relief and now the game
could begin. Arkansas High had won the coin toss before the game
and had elected to defer to the second half and Bentonvile had
chosen to receive the opening kick off. Both teams were very
tentative in the first few series of the game. At the end of the first
quarter the game was still a scoreless tie. Both teams had had
difficulty getting any offense started. The players seemed very
jittery and spent most of the first quarter getting nerves under
control. The second quarter began with a couple of completed short
out-routes by the Bentonville quarterback which put them near mid-
field. The following play the Bentonville quarterback turned to hand
the ball off to the big half-back they had. As he hit the line he was
stood up and Blake Brady came in from the side hitting the running
back and knocked the ball loose. Keith dove for the ball and
bounced off his pads and was sent tumbling down the mid-field
stripe. Two Bentonville players pounced on the ball along with
Blake Brady who was still scrambling. The Bentonville players had
beaten Blake to the ball. The crowd let out a sigh realizing the ball
would remain with Bentonville, but as the players un-piled Blake

emerged with the ball and the official signaled Arkansas High football. Arkansas High coaches stunned, turned quickly to send the offense onto the field. Arkansas High players jumping, slapping high-fives made their way to the sideline with several of them patting Blake on the back and slapping his back. As he made his way to the sideline Doc leaned over and said, "Hey son of a gun, that's the way to get in the pile and fight for that ball. You were the last one on the pile and ball was at the bottom." Brady then turned to Doc and grinned from ear to ear and said, "As I hit the pile Coach I couldn't see the ball, because it was already covered up. I felt for the ball, and I kept rooting around for it until I had it. When I did I just squeezed her like she was mine and pulled her away from everybody else. By the time we un-piled I had it."

Jamie and the rest of the offense made their way onto the field. The first play was a handoff to McAfee. He followed George's blocking and picked up four yards. They lined up for the second down, Jamie turned the snap and turned and pitched the ball to McAfee. The defensive end immediately read the play and was in the back field to drag McAfee down for a three yard loss. It was now third and nine and the crowd came to its feet. Jamie took the snap and rolled out to his right and was able to spot Knight between two defenders. Jamie quickly unloaded the ball then Knight made a catch seven yards down the field. The defensive back then hit him and Knight dragged him for another three yards to pick up the first down. The chains were moved for the first down and a play was brought in from the sideline. Cleveland called and off-tackle hand-off to McAfee again. Jamie looked at the players in the huddle, hesitated a second and looked around then said, "Okay, they're expecting another handoff. Let's fake the handoff to McAfee. McAfee give me a good fake. Dive into the line like you've got the ball. I'm going to take it around the left end. Knight, you line up at left wide out. Get the cornerback out of the play, just whatever you have to do, get him to the sideline." Jamie went up to the line of scrimmage and called out the signals. He turned and faked the handoff to McAfee who doubled over selling the fake as he went into the line. He was stacked up and piled for what Bentonville thought was a play with no gain. Then Jamie rolled around the right end at a slow trot with the ball on his hip as if he was just closing out the play. He looked up and saw an opening, tucked the ball and took off. The free safety and the cornerback were the only players with a chance at Jamie. Knight saw Jamie coming and quickly turned to block the cornerback and seal him off from the play. Jamie raced down the sideline to the 15 when the free safety finally caught up with him. Jamie tried to stop and reverse his field but the safety got enough of an arm on Jamie to cause him to stumble. He stumbled forward for another five yards trying with all of his being to stay off of the ground, but finally fell down at the ten yard line. The Arkansas High crowd and bench jumped to their feet cheering wildly. Jamie then walked back to the huddle with the rest of the players slapping him on his back. The play was sent into the huddle. Jamie lined the team up and again handed the ball off to McAfee behind Farmer. Kyle Farmer cleared a path and McAfee fought down to the four yard line. It was second down and four. Arkansas High packed the line tight. Bentonville brought in some of the bigger defensive players to beef up their defensive line and make a goal line stand. Bentonville was looking for another play right up the middle to McAfee. They had done well running to him all night and they counted on him to be called on again. Jamie called out the signals and the team fired off the line and a pile of humanity came together creating one great wall on the four yard line. Jamie took the snap and turned and pitched the ball to McAfee who scampered around the left end with Farmer leading the blocking. Farmer looked up trying to find anyone to block but the Bentonville defense was piled up in the middle of the field. McAfee could have walked into the end zone behind Farmer but he quickly scampered across the goal line to put Arkansas ahead 6 to 0. With the extra point the score was now 7 to 0.

With six minutes left in the second quarter Arkansas High kicked the ball to Bentonville. The first two plays were running plays. Each was smothered by the defense. Bentonville now faced a third and eight yards to go. The quarterback dropped back to pass. The defensive line quickly broke through and was right in the in quarterback's face. He suddenly shot a screen pass to the running back coming out of the back field. The pass was caught and the back broke a tackle and scampered all the way to the 50 yard line before being dragged down from behind. Suddenly Bentonville had some momentum. They continued to drive down the field. With two minutes and eight seconds left before half time they punched the ball into the end zone making the score 7 to 6. Bentonville then added the extra point to tie the score.

Bentonville lined up following the touchdown. Dee turned to Cleveland and said, "So do we just run out the clock or do we try to score?" Cleveland paused briefly, "Uh, let's do this. Let's try a running play then a few short passes and see if we can get down the field a little bit. If we are moving the ball we'll go ahead and try to score. But if those first few plays don't work we'll make sure we don't give 'em the ball back with any time on the clock. I can handle going into half time tied, but I don't want to go into half time down 7. Right now their offense has some momentum. If we give 'em the ball with enough time to score we're in trouble." "Sounds simple," Dee said. Cleveland scowled, "We'll see how simple it is." Files turned to the coaches, "How many time outs do we have?" "One," grunted Cleveland. "Ooh, I like these odds," said Files as he smiled and walked away.

As the ball was kicked Jamie walked over to Cleveland. Cleveland turned and said, "Alright Bridges," we've got only a couple of minutes before half. We have to burn the clock. I don't want three passes then out then punting from our own ten yard line with a minute and forty left on the clock. That will give their offense too much time to work with, alright?" "No problem," Jamie replied. "Score or kill the clock," he continued. The ball was kicked off and bounced into the end zone for a touch back. Jamie went into the huddle and called the play Cleveland had given him. The offense moved to the line. The Bentonville defense had a rekindled fire after scoring to even the game. The defensive players stunted and shifted as Jamie barked out the signals. He turned to give the ball to McAfee who took the handoff and was met at the line by a host of Bentonville defenders. The new fire kindled in the defense was now a full blown blaze after stuffing McAfee. The time continued to click off the clock as the next play was brought into the huddle. Cleveland turned to Dee, "We try this little pass. If it works we keep doing it. If not we run to McAfee and get the clock down to nothing." The teams lined up. Jamie took the snap and dropped back to pass. The Bentonville defense was immediately in his face and he evaded one tackler and tried to run around the left end. As he got to the corner the left defensive end jumped on him and rolled him to the ground for a three yard loss. Before much time could tick off the clock Bentonville called a time out. "Dad gum it!" Cleveland shouted. "They still have a time out left too. So they stop us here on third and they get the ball near mid-field with over a minute left." Jamie trotted to the sideline, "What do we do?" "What do we do?!" Cleveland shouted back, "I told you what to do two minutes ago. We either score or run the clock out and you said 'no problem'! So, Mr. No Problem, what do we do?" Jamie paused a moment and just as he began to answer, Cleveland then shouted, "We have no choice! We run the ball and then make them take their last time out. If the pass is incomplete not only do they have the ball with a minute left they have a time out too." The official blew the whistle. The players got back onto the field. Jamie then asked urgently, "So what are we running?" "Oh, run the ball!" screamed Cleveland. Jamie looked a little puzzled and then ran quickly back onto the field. He walked into the huddle and said, "Jamie Special." He looked at Knight, "Split out to the right end, run a flag to that side. Take as many as you can with you." The players came to the line of scrimmage. Time was ticking down on the play clock and Jamie hurriedly called out the signals and took the snap. He turned right keeping the ball in his right hand but behind his back. He brushed past Farmer gently sliding the ball into his stomach. He reached with his left hand, which was in front of him, to give the impression he was giving the ball to McAfee. McAfee doubled over hard and hit the line and was stacked up. Jamie then rolled to the right as if he had the ball on his hip like a few plays earlier. Jamie continued to roll and look as if he was trying to find Knight down field to throw to. Farmer stayed crouched in the backfield pretending he was trying to cut off the back side from getting to Jamie and providing some blocking. The entire line shifted to the right then Farmer took off. He ripped through the line to the left side. As he broke past the line of scrimmage he ran head long into the offensive cornerback on that side trying to get across the field to where Jamie was scampering. The cornerback was as surprised as anybody to get hit by Farmer and laid on the ground. Farmer stumbled then righted himself and then took off again. He broke from there and flew down the field with all the speed he could muster. The safety suddenly realized what had happened and quickly turned to run Farmer down. He crossed mid field with Farmer still far enough ahead but the safety had and angle and was gaining. At the 15 yard line the safety lunged toward Farmer who stuck out a stiff arm. The safety latched on to Farmer's arm and shoulder. The battle of wills was now taking place and when it came to a battle of wills I'd want Farmer on my side every time. He instead of trying to tear away from the safety, clinched his fist near the neck of the kid's jersey and tugged once down to the seven yard line and then tugged and dragged him down to the four and with one giant heave drug the defender into the end zone. The stadium erupted. Farmer and the Bentonville player both lay in the end zone like two prize fighters after a fifteen round battle trying to get their breath back. The rest of the offense quickly ran into the end zone picking Farmer up and jumped and screamed. The players ran off the field celebrating. As the players ran to the bench Jamie eased past Cleveland and said, "No problem." Cleveland smiled and shouted back, "There's still almost a minute left on the clock." Jamie then shot back, "You said 'OR'. You said 'run the clock out OR score' Had you said 'AND', 'run the clock out AND score' I would not have said 'no problem'." Attention suddenly turned back to the field as they lined up for the extra point. The ball was snapped and bounced back to Knight who was the holder. He tried to put the ball on the block so it could be kicked but he never was able to get it down. Knight stood up with the ball and called "FIRE" which is a signal for the players to go out for a pass if there is a bad snap, so that they can convert possibly a two point conversion if the holder is in trouble. Knight scooped up the ball up, rolled to his left then quickly was wrestled to the ground by the Bentonville players. The celebration for Arkansas High was suddenly blunted as the score after the missed conversion was now 13 to 7. Arkansas High then kicked the ball off. The defense came onto the field and was able to hold Bentonville in check until the final seconds of the half ticked off.

Some of the sophomores entered the locker room celebrating, but the majority of the players realized that this game was very far from over. Cleveland called all the coaches together and began, "Alright, let's first break into offensive and defensive groups. Go over adjustments but leave me five minutes at the end. I want to get 'em back together and get 'em pumped up before the second half." The players broke into groups. The offense gathered in the front of the locker room while the defense gathered in the back. Both groups went over adjustments. As the Bentonville band finished playing faintly over the noise of the coaches you could hear the announcer speaking over the intercom. He said, "Folks, before the Arkansas High band plays I want to give you an update on other playoff games of interest." At that moment the locker room became silent. "At the half," the announcer continued, "El Dorado leads 17 to 3". A big cheer went up from the Arkansas High crowd, most realizing that Arkansas High had already beaten El Dorado this season. After the silence, the coaches kind of all looked around to each other as if to say 'this is our state championship game' then began talking to the players again. At the end of the group sessions the team gathered back together as a whole Cleveland walked to the front of the team. "Men," he began, "apparently this is the state championship game tonight. We already know we can beat El Dorado. If we can pull off a win tonight we'll beat those Wildcats again, if they win and it sounds like they will." "Men," he continued, "don't come back into this locker room with any regrets. Put everything you have on that field and let's go win this game." The players ran out of the locker room and back onto the field. The crowd was cheering wildly, the band was playing. By the end of the third quarter the score was still 13 to 7 in favor of Arkansas High, but Bentonville was driving. At the quarter change Bentonville had the ball on the Arkansas High 10 yard line. Doc met with the defensive players on the sideline during the break between quarters. He said, "Look men, them son of a guns can't have anything. If you give them this suddenly they got that fire and it's going to be a heck of a battle to put that fire out. You line up and bust them harder than you ever hit any son of a gun. If you stop 'em here you'll demoralize them and the offense, they won't get us another score. You demoralize these boys, let our offense score and we go to Little Rock next week.

The players re-entered the field of play. Along the line of scrimmage there was grunting and growling as the signals were being called. Suddenly the ball was snapped and Arkansas High defensive line tore through the line and was quickly in the face of the quarterback. He while back pedaling, dumped the ball over the middle of the line to his tight end who had drifted into the middle of the field for a screen pass. He made the catch at the six yard line and quickly ran down to the one where he was hit and bounced off the tackler into the end zone making the score 13 to 13. Bentonville then added the extra point to lead now 14 to 13. The first half of the third quarter was chewed up with Arkansas High driving down to the Bentonville 45 and then having to punt on a third and eight. Bentonville took over on their own ten yard line. Mixing running plays and passing plays Bentonville made it down to the Arkansas High 15 but was faced with a third down and 6 with 5 minutes and 5 seconds remaining in the game. Bentonville came to the line of scrimmage and Cleveland called out to the players, "Watch the tight end screen!" It seemed as if none of the players could hear him over the crowd and all the excitement of the game. The ball was snapped and again the Arkansas High line was immediately in the quarterback's face. Cleveland at this point realized it was again the tight end screen, the same play that they were burned on for the previous touchdown. "Dad gum it!" Cleveland screamed. "We're falling for it again!" he continued. The pass was dropped over the middle right into the tight end's hands. The tight end caught the pass and turned to look up field. Suddenly there was a loud crunch and the tight end was on the ground without the ball. Blake Brady was on top of him. Blake had heard Cleveland and had not rushed He stood his ground, and as soon as the tight end caught the ball Blake flew to him and hit him with the velocity of a small missile. There was suddenly a scramble for the ball. Bentonville was able to recover but it was back at their own 17 yard line. The field goal team came in on the field and was able to put Bentonville up 17 to 13 with 2 minutes and 13 seconds remaining on the clock. The Bentonville side of the stadium celebrated as if the game was over and danced in the stands. The ball was kicked off and Arkansas High was able to return it to the 35 yard line. Jamie quickly navigated the offense down the field mostly by passing the ball mixed in with an occasional running play. 43 seconds were left on the clock and Arkansas High had driven down to the 16 yard line with facing a third and 6. Files turned to Cleveland, "Run or pass?" "We have to pass," responded Cleveland. "We have one time out left but we need save it." Knight ran onto the field with the play. It was to be a pass to the tight end, Ryan Doster. Jamie took the snap, dropped back and Ryan broke into a clearing just beyond the line of scrimmage. Jamie reared back and released the ball. At the line of scrimmage the ball was batted down by one of the Bentonville linemen. Cleveland turned to Files, "Run that play again. It's there! It's there! Just tell Bridges roll out a little further this time." The play was brought to the huddle. It was now fourth down and six on the 16 yard line with 37 seconds left on the clock. Jamie took the snap and he rolled right, Doster again broke into a clearing. Jamie threw the pass. This time it cleared the line. As the ball came into Doster's hands he was immediately met by a Bentonville defensive player and the ball was knocked from his hands before he could gain full possession. It was over. Suddenly the season had come to an end. The ball lay on the ground and the players stood stunned. The Bentonville defense raced off the field celebrating while the Arkansas High team and coaches and fans stood in stunned silence. The offense made its way onto the field and the defense walked onto the field and Bentonville just downed the ball and allowed the time to run off the clock.

The final horn blew and reality set in. The fans who had brought snack cakes with them threw them onto the track. George and a few of the other sophomores gathered up the boxes. George was grateful to them and smiled but felt like a part of him had died inside. He picked them up with none of the excitement he had in previous games. He wanted so much just to leave them there and just walk away but he thought it would be disrespectful to the people who had bought them for him and brought them. Several of the sophomores helped him with the rest of the boxes. Each week the number had grown and grown and now there were several hundred boxes laying on the field. The other players just sat or lay crying on the field. Keith lay in a fetal position where the last play had ended, crying. The coaches got the players up and got them together so that they could shake hands with the Bentonville team then hurried them into the locker room. The players entered the locker rooms crying and slamming doors. Jamie stood quietly in front of his locker. Keith sat crying in front of his. Blake Brady stood calmly undressing with tears rolling down his face. Cleveland walked to the front of the locker room, "Men, I'm proud of you. If you had told me we'd be here tonight at the beginning of the season I'd have never believed you. Man, I was just hoping this team could break .500. I know you're hurting, but you have played so far above your head all year you have nothing to be ashamed of. I want you to know I'll never forget what you did this season. I'll never forget this team. Men, there are only four teams in our state classification who played football tonight. You were one of those four. Men, you were very close to being only one of those two that are playing next week. You are very fine football team and you've grown to be fine young men." With that Cleveland walked out of the locker room with the rest of the coaching staff.

When the coaches had left the locker room Keith screamed, "But we weren't good enough! We lost! It's over! It was all a waste!" Jamie jumped to his feet, "A loss, yeah. I'll give you that Keith, and it hurts. It hurts me as bad as it does anybody. But it wasn't a waste. I can guarantee you that. Life's not about the goal, it's about the journey. The majority of life is spent on our journey towards something. Even if you reach the goal whatever you get for making it to that goal is usually short lived. Had we won tonight the goal would have been one more Friday night, but the journey was all season. You know what I saw on my journey?" Keith looked up with a scowl on his face and said, "What?" Jamie continued, "Keith, I saw myself being accepted by a group of guys who didn't even know me, including you, and now I call you all my friends. This journey has led me to a new group of friends and it led me to a man who became like a father to me, although he passed away. I'll always remember him as a father to me. Keith, you know what I saw in you? I saw you go from a cocky little punk linebacker who couldn't take a hit without coming out of the game early in the season to be anchor of our defensive line. You became the one the entire team would rally around. You know what I saw as a team? I saw us go from being a bunch of self-centered little losers to a real team. Keith, you know as well as I do that we didn't have near the talent that Bentonville or El Dorado have. But you know as well as I do that on any given night we could beat 'em because we play as a team." George suddenly interrupted, "Hey, Jamie. I saw that there was more to life than food, or even football. Guy's I'm taking all of this food to the homeless shelter tonight. During this season I learned that I can help others, and man before the season started all I wanted to do was help myself. Help myself to any food I could get, but now I've found out it's even better to go and help others. Man, you gotta see these kids at the shelter. When I come in they think I'm their hero. They think I'm some kind of Santa Claus or something. I play with them, I give them food, man, they go crazy! Guys I tell ya, I wanted to win state as bad as anybody. And it hurts, oh, I promise you, it hurts. But this season was without that win was still the best time in my life I've ever had. I learned more this season from the game of football than I ever learned in any school book." Some of the guys started murmuring and talking and suddenly Blake Brady stood up and turned from his locker and began to speak. The room went totally silent when Brady began to speak because it was so rare to ever hear him talk much. He had not spoken in front of the team the entire year. He had talked to different players but never addressed the entire team. He began, "You know what fellas? I'm going to Heaven because of this football season." Some of the players looked puzzled and he continued, "You guys know me. You know what my life has been. You know where I come from. Most of you have seen my uncle's crack house where I live, where I stay. You know my family is gone. But hey! It's all okay, you know why? Because I've got a family right here around me. I consider you guys as much of a family as I've ever had in my entire life. You know some people would say this is sad, but you guys are the only people in the whole world that would give a rat if I died tomorrow. It's kinda weird, but if I died tomorrow and we had to have a funeral for me next week you would be the people sitting in that family section of the funeral home. But you know what? I couldn't be more proud to have you sitting in that family section. There would be no greater honor for me to know that ya'll had sat there. Oh, yeah. And by the way, I may live in the crummiest crack house in town, but when I die I gotta mansion at the end of a street of gold because some of my family, you guys, told me about Jesus. This season a waste? Nah! You may feel that way Keith, my friend, but for me, it was the greatest time in my whole life." Tears began to stream down Brady's face as he sat down at his locker. He looked up and said, "By far, the greatest time in my life was the last four months." He put his head down, several of the players came by and slapped him on the back. The players began to take off equipment and uniforms, pile the pads into their locker and throw the game clothes into a pile so the coaches could wash them.

The players filed one by one out of the locker room. Some had gotten dressed quickly and eased out while others had taken their time. Each one would open the door into the cool night air where just minutes before it was electric with excitement of one of the best games ever played at that stadium. George walked out with Bridges and Brady and McAfee, all four of them carrying all the boxes of snack cakes their arms could hold and loaded them into George's vehicle. "You sure you don't want to go with me?" George asked the others. "Aw, don't want to steal your thunder Santa Claus," Jamie replied. McAfee kind of nodded then Brady said, "Hey, hey, George, I don't have anywhere to go." Brady seemed almost nervous. "Can I tag along?" he asked. "Sure," said George, "Come on. The more the merrier!" The two climbed into George's vehicle and sped away. Jamie and McAfee stood in the empty parking lot. "Wow," McAfee said. "What?" Jamie asked. "Are those the same two guys we started the season with?" "What do you mean?" Jamie replied. "Well," said McAfee, "in the yearbook Brady probably would have been voted most likely to be in jail and George would have been the most likely to eat every buffet in town out of business. Now look at them." Jamie thought a minute and then replied, "You know, Jerome, we all have hang-ups. We all got something that makes our life a struggle. But do you know what's cool?" "What?" McAfee asked. "When you put all of us out there on that field with all our weaknesses and faults, it's almost like the strength that we have cover each guy's weakness and instead of being a big mass of faults and problems and weaknesses, we're the opposite. We're almost the best team in the state. You know, McAfee, there are times when I get up to that line of scrimmage and just knowing how well you run, and and how well George can block, well it gives me more confidence in myself and so my weaknesses kind of go away. You know George and Brady, man those were guys that before the season all you could see was their faults. And that's all they had. That's all anybody ever could see. But during this season they both found something to hang their hat on. Brady found this team and found Jesus, and then George, well George found that he could be useful, that he could help people.

That's all those guys needed. That English teacher, Mrs. Johnson, she always says that football is a waste of time and money. A couple of weeks ago in class she was going on and on about how much money has been spent on football and how little spent on school. But you know what? I look at this team and see what a difference football made in their lives, especially guys like Brady and George. You know their life's going to be different because of one thing, and that one thing is one fall of football."

Made in the USA
Middletown, DE
18 December 2017